Detectives in Togas

Detectives
in Togas

HENRY WINTERFELD

Illustrated by Charlotte Kleinert

Translated from the German by
Richard and Clara Winston

HARCOURT BRACE & COMPANY

Orlando   Atlanta   Austin   Boston   San Francisco   Chicago   Dallas   New York
Toronto   London

This edition is published by special arrangement with Harcourt Brace
& Company.

For permission to reprint copyrighted material, grateful acknowledgment is
made to the following sources:

Harcourt Brace & Company: Detectives in Togas by Henry Winterfield,
translated by Richard and Clara Winston, illustrated by Charlotte Kleinert.
Copyright © 1956 by Henry Winterfield, renewed 1984 by K. Winston and
J. W. Gregory.

Deborah Nourse Lattimore: Cover illustration by Deborah Nourse
Lattimore from *Detectives in Togas* by Henry Winterfield.

Printed in the United States of America

ISBN 0-15-305232-5

4 5 6 7 8 9 10   060   97 96

*During the 1936 excavations in Pompeii a temple
wall came to light on which had been scribbled, in a
childish hand, the words:*

CAIUS ASINUS EST

*That scrawl from the days of Ancient Rome was the
inspiration for this book.*

CONTENTS

Detectives in Togas

1

The Wrong Lantern

Mucius raised his head in surprise. The entire class had suddenly gone off into gales of laughter, and he did not know why. He had been concentrating on his work and had not noticed what was happening in the classroom. Now he saw that Rufus had left his seat and was standing near the wall, behind their teacher, Xantippus. He must have sneaked past the teacher—quite a trick if you could get away with it. Hanging from a big nail on the wall was a map of the Roman Empire, and on this nail Rufus had hung one of his wax writing tablets. He had scratched on it in big, crooked letters:

CAIUS IS A DUMBBELL

The joke went over big because Caius really was not very bright. Rufus grinned and bowed like an actor on the stage. Xantippus, who had been read-

CAIUS

RUFUS

ing, looked up in consternation. "Quiet!" he said in a voice of thunder.

Instantly there was silence. Rufus ducked his head in alarm, and the others made a show of bending over their work. A while ago they had been reciting Greek words: *ho georgos*, the farmer; *ho lukos*, the wolf; *ho dendron*, the tree; *ho hippos*, the horse, and so on. They were then supposed to write the words from memory. So now they went back to their tablets. Mucius whispered to Antonius, who sat next to him, "What's the matter with Rufus? He's stirring up trouble for himself."

Antonius grinned. "He's mad at Caius," he whispered back. "Caius wouldn't let him study. He kept poking him in the back with his stylus."

ANTONIUS MUCIUS

Mucius frowned. He had warned Caius again and again not to bother the others. Mucius was the class monitor and the boys were supposed to mind him. But Caius didn't like minding anybody. Perhaps he thought he didn't have to because his father was the wealthy senator Vinicius.

Caius was rough and strong, but he was not really mean; he had a weakness for practical jokes. The trouble was he didn't like it a bit when the joke was on him. His face had turned bright red when Rufus hung up the sign. Now, finally, he lost all control of himself. "And you're the son of a coward!" he bellowed at Rufus.

Xantippus looked up again, dumbfounded. "I am the son of a coward?" he asked, frowning. "What

3

FLAVIUS | JULIUS | PUBLIUS

do you mean by that?" Before Caius could explain, the whole room was in an uproar.

Rufus adored his father, and Caius' insulting words had touched a tender spot: his father, Marcus Praetonius, was a famous general, but he had just recently lost an important battle somewhere in Gaul, and Rufus felt deeply humiliated. "You're a liar!" he shouted, and made a rush at Caius.

Caius was knocked backward, along with his bench. Grappling, the two boys rolled on the floor, while the others jumped up on their benches to get a better view of the fracas. This was as good as any gladiator fight in the arena.

Suddenly Xantippus took command of the situation. He went over to the boys, managed to get

between them and pulled them to their feet. Panting, Caius and Rufus glared at one another. Rufus' tunic was ripped at the collar, and Caius' toga had gathered up most of the dirt from the floor. As for Xantippus, he was furious. "Mucius!" he said, breathing heavily from the effort of separating the fighters, "what in the world brought on this disgusting conduct? Fighting in school! Disgraceful!"

Xantippus was a Greek, and his real name was Xanthos. Xantippus was only a nickname the boys had given him because he reminded them of Xantippe, the wife of the famous philosopher Socrates, who was always bad-tempered and nagged her husband. The boys thought their teacher also was a terrible nagger. He always insisted on "hard work and perfect conduct." Unlike most teachers, however, he never beat the boys; he had other ways of making them respect him. He had some peculiar ideas, too—for example, he would not allow the slaves who brought the boys to school to stay on during the lessons, as was the custom. Xantippus made the slaves leave and come back for the boys in the evening. Boys could not keep their minds on their studies when there were others around, he said.

What was more, Xantippus was in a position to lay down the law in such matters. He was a famous mathematician who had written many books about circles, triangles, diagonals, parallelograms, and suchlike head-splitting stuff. His school, known as the Xanthos School, was one of the finest grammar schools in Rome. Only wealthy patricians could afford to send their sons to it. For that reason Xantippus' classes were generally small. At present the school consisted of only seven boys: Mucius, Caius, Rufus, Publius, Julius, Flavius and Antonius. All of them happened to live fairly close together in a neighborhood of elegant mansions on the Esquiline Hill.

Xantippus was still waiting for Mucius to account for the fight. "What's the matter with you?" he snapped. "Have you lost your tongue?"

Mucius pulled himself together. "I can't say how it happened," he said hesitantly. "I was writing the Greek words and wasn't paying attention to much else."

Xantippus couldn't very well find fault with Mucius for that.

"We were all doing our work," Antonius rashly offered.

Xantippus became suspicious. He bore down on Rufus and said, "Show me your list of Greek words immediately!"

"I . . . I haven't done one," Rufus stammered.

"Why not?" Xantippus demanded icily.

"I . . . I was having writer's cramp," Rufus murmured feebly.

It was a silly excuse, but the boys thought Rufus was a good sport for not telling on Caius. He could have said that Caius' pestering had kept him from writing.

"Indeed? Writer's cramp?" Xantippus repeated with evident disbelief. He turned to Caius. "And what about you?" he asked.

"Me?" Caius pretended amazement.

"Yes, you! You think I mean Romulus and Remus? Where is your word list?"

"I have none," Caius mumbled, shrugging.

"Why not?"

"I just couldn't remember any of them." Caius sighed. He seemed almost offended that Xantippus should expect him to remember.

"I'll teach you a lesson you'll not forget!" Xantippus snorted. "Fighting in class instead of attending to your work! Which one of you started it?"

Caius and Rufus did not reply.

"Aha!" Xantippus said. "So you want to be heroes, eh? You force me to take severe measures." He pointed his forefinger like a drawn dagger at Rufus and asked slyly, "Well, what were you doing at the wall behind my back? Speak, Rufus Marcus Praetonius!"

Still Rufus did not answer. He merely gawked at his teacher.

Xantippus whirled around and scanned the wall. He caught sight of the writing tablet on which was scribbled *"Caius is a Dumbbell"* and exploded. "Ha! So that is what you were up to! I thought you had writer's cramp. You just wait, my boy. I see you don't know me. You've been fooling around instead of working. You've raised a rumpus in the classroom. And on top of it all you've lied to me. Pack your things at once and go! The Xanthos School is no wrestling ring for undisciplined young Romans. Tomorrow I shall see your mother and ask her to withdraw you from the school. I'll return the money she has paid for your tuition. You are not worth all your parents are spending on you."

After this outburst he ordered the others to return to their seats and get to work. But he had not forgotten Caius. "And as for you, tomorrow you will bring in the whole assignment with every word in the list written ten times in your best handwriting!" he snapped. "And woe betide you if I find a single mistake."

Without another word, Xantippus returned to his desk where he became absorbed in his book. He did not deign to look at Rufus. Caius sat down, flushed with anger. But Rufus stood petrified, staring in horror at the teacher. The others stole glances at him. Rufus had always been particularly proud of being a student at the famous Xanthos School. His parents placed great hopes in him. The high tuition fee was a real burden for them, for his father was far from rich. It took a great deal of money to equip his legions.

Suddenly Rufus ran up to the teacher's desk and cried out imploringly:

"Please don't go to my mother tomorrow! Punish me some other way, but not that."

Xantippus waved him irritably aside. "Your repentance comes too late," he grumbled. He did not even look up from his book. Behind the outstretched roll of papyrus only his tousled gray hair and pointed beard could be seen.

Slowly, Rufus walked back to his bench and gathered up his school equipment, which had fallen to the floor during his fight with Caius. During the brawl Mucius' lantern had also fallen to the floor, and he had forgotten to pick it up. It was a handsome bronze lantern with his name, Mucius Marius Domitius, engraved on it. Rufus packed it up with the rest of his things, not realizing his own lantern had rolled under another bench. Mucius noticed the mistake, but he did not want to trouble Rufus about it now.

After he had finished packing up, Rufus slowly put on his mantle. It was a homespun woolen cloak, somewhat too short for him. The mantle had a long tear on the left shoulder which had been neatly darned with darker wool.

Rufus gave one last, pleading look at Xantippus, who refused to take further notice of him. Then he unhappily stepped out into the street. The Xanthos School was located on Broad Street, a bustling, busy avenue by day. Nearby was the crowded Roman Forum with its orator's platform and its many public buildings, temples, and monuments. The Forum was famous throughout the world; everyone thought of it as the heart of the Roman Empire.

Because Broad Street was an elegant business street, Xantippus had considered it a desirable location for his school. He had rented a small house for that purpose. The schoolroom was on the ground floor and open for its entire width on the street side, so that the boys were practically on public display. But they had long ago become accustomed to that, and passersby paid little attention to them. The sight of pupils at their studies was quite familiar; many low-cost schools, in fact, were held in public arcades.

The Xanthos School was not exactly popular in the neighborhood. Lessons began before sunrise, and the voices of the boys at their recitations woke people from their sleep. But there was nothing to be done about that. After all, the boys were not attending school for their own pleasure, but in order to become educated men and fine citizens.

Rufus started down Broad Street toward the Forum. But he paused at the first corner, and then took a seat on a wine barrel which was chained to the wall in front of a tavern. Mucius, from his bench in school, could see Rufus plainly and wondered why he was sitting there so long. Had he already forgotten his troubles? He seemed to be showing a lively interest in the throng on the street.

The sun had set behind the Janiculus Hill and it was growing dark. A few stars could already be seen in the cloudless sky. Broad Street was jammed with people, most of whom came from the nearby baths on the Field of Mars. Their sandals slapped against the stone pavement. Scraps of conversation and laughter could now and then be distinguished from the hum of voices. Beggars crouching by the curb pleaded with passersby for alms. A few street peddlers shouted themselves hoarse trying to dispose of their wares before dark—hot sausages, figs dipped in honey, olives, fruit cakes, and other tidbits at bargain prices. A detachment of the Praetorian Guard, wearing chest armor and shouldering bamboo lances, marched past in military order, led by a young officer with sword and plumed helmet. Right behind them came a large farm wagon drawn by two sturdy mules. It was piled high with produce. Its clumsy wheels made a deafening racket on the rough pavement. The wagon stopped just in front of the school, for approaching it from the other direction came a sedan chair carried by eight Negroes in magnificent livery. The street was blocked, and instantly a crowd gathered. The runner, who was clearing the way for the sedan chair, struck out rudely with his stick, shouting, "Make room for His Excellency! Make room for His Excellency!"

The crowd drew back, and the farmer drove his wagon halfway up onto the narrow sidewalk in order to give the sedan chair room to pass. Inside the chair sat a fat, bald-headed man wearing a senator's toga with two red bands. He was reading a book and fanning himself with an Oriental fan. Apparently he was a very high dignitary, for he had an unusually large following of slaves and admirers. The people on the street called out loud greetings to him, and some even rushed up to kiss his hands. Others cracked jokes that called forth roars of laughter.

When the fat man looked up, Mucius recognized him by the large scar that ran diagonally across his bald pate. He was Ex-consul Tellus. Many years ago he had been a top-ranking general. Now he was supposed to be living in luxurious retirement on the many millions he had made out of the booty of his successful campaigns.

As the Negroes trotted on with the sedan chair, Tellus waved his fan graciously at the crowd. Then he disappeared from Mucius' sight. The farm wagon started up again and lumbered off toward the Forum.

Lucky that heavy wagons aren't allowed into the city by day, Mucius thought. *With the streets so narrow, they would be bottling up traffic all the time.*

Now there was really nothing left to see. The bustle on the street was beginning to quiet down; only a few stragglers hastened by, obviously intending to get home as quickly as possible before nightfall. The beggars and peddlers had disappeared. Two night watchmen with long staffs over their shoulders came into sight across the street. They sauntered from shop to shop, making sure that the shutters in front of each were well locked.

Rufus was still sitting on the wine barrel, staring into space. Perhaps he was waiting for school to let out, when the slaves would come along to take the boys home. They were due any moment now. But suddenly he sprang to his feet, sped across the street and disappeared around a corner into a side street that led past the Field of Mars to the big bridge across the Tiber.

Mucius, watching, thought this odd behavior. If Rufus intended to go home, he would have to cross the Forum—but he was heading in the opposite direction. It was already quite late; the first hour of the night had begun, and nobody liked walking through the totally dark streets alone at night.

"I suppose he just means to go by a roundabout way," Mucius said to himself. "He certainly won't be in a hurry to see his mother tonight."

This seemed as good an explanation as any, and Mucius at last applied himself to that dull list of Greek words. Within a few minutes all thought of Rufus was gone from his mind.

2

A Muffled Groan

The next morning when the boys arrived at school, Xantippus was not there. This was reason for wonder—their teacher had never kept them waiting before.

They had arrived punctually an hour before sunrise and taken their seats on the benches as they were supposed to do. The slaves had accompanied them only as far as the Forum, since they had to go shopping in the markets. Rufus, of course, was absent, and so was Caius. Only Mucius, Julius, Flavius, Publius and Antonius had showed up, and they could not figure out why Caius was missing. Perhaps he had not done his homework and was playing hookey for that reason, though that would hardly help him. Xantippus had an excellent memory, especially when it came to punishments.

But where could Xantippus be? Not that the boys were so eager to see him, but it was dull sitting here in silence and staring at the walls. They were cold and sleepy and would much rather have been home in bed. Their lanterns, which they had placed on the benches beside them, flickered dimly and smelled of burnt olive oil. It was still dusky outside; in the gray predawn, Broad Street was lifeless and deserted.

Silently, Antonius and Flavius chewed a couple of rolls which they had bought at the baker's on their way to school, since they had left home before breakfast. But gradually the boys became uneasy. Xantippus' living quarters adjoined the schoolroom, separated from it only by a thin curtain. If Xantippus were up, the boys certainly ought to hear him. But all was silence behind the curtain.

"He's overslept," Publius said, grinning maliciously.

Julius shook his head. "Out of the question," he said. "Xantippus always gets up before the tenth hour of the night. He's told us that himself."

"I don't believe everything he says," Publius scoffed.

Flavius suggested that Xantippus might have gone to pay an early visit to Rufus' mother. But Mucius growled, "Rot! Nobody but a schoolboy goes anywhere before dawn. Put out your lantern. The smoke is choking me."

Flavius blew out his lantern. Antonius suddenly noticed that Xantippus' stool lay on the floor, tipped over in front of the desk. This was puzzling, for Xantippus always kept the room in perfect order.

"Maybe he's sick," Julius said.

"What would that have to do with the stool?" Publius asked.

"Otherwise he would have picked it up," Julius replied. "We had better go in and see what's the matter with him."

Mucius objected. "If Xantippus is sick he would already have called us. We'll wait."

"All right." Publius yawned. "I'm happy as long as he lets us alone." He stretched out on the bench and made believe he was snoring.

The others laughed. But Antonius gave them a fright by exclaiming in a tense voice: "Maybe Xantippus has been murdered!"

Flavius paled. He was not much of a hero. Involuntarily he turned to look at the curtain.

"Who would want to murder Xantippus?" Mucius demanded realistically.

"Lukos!" Antonius whispered.

Antonius was always one for expecting the worst. His head was full of ghosts and criminals. Every night before going to sleep he looked under his bed to see whether any burglars were lurking there, but he was always disappointed. His friends knew all about his tendency to imagine things. But this time they were impressed. The mention of Lukos made them all shudder a little.

Lukos was a famous astrologist and seer. Supposedly he came from Alexandria, the great Greek colony in Egypt. He had turned up in Rome about two years ago. All kinds of stories went around about him. He was supposed to have mysterious powers, for he had predicted a great many important political events. Rumor had it that he could also work magic.

The boys were fascinated by Lukos because his house stood directly across the street from the school and they could watch it all the time. It was a gloomy, windowless building made of heavy stone blocks; it towered over the low shops to either side of it. Beside the imposing front door hung a sign on which was written in big, bright-red letters:

LUKOS,
WORLD-FAMOUS ASTROLOGIST,
MEMBER OF THE ACADEMY OF ALEXANDRIA,
FORMER PERSONAL SOOTHSAYER TO THE KING OF
PERSIA.
OFFICE HOURS: AFTER SUNSET.
BEGGARS AND PEDDLERS KEEP OUT!
MORTAL DANGER!

The boys had read the sign again and again, but it thrilled them anew every time they saw it. Especially the last line: MORTAL DANGER! Antonius imagined that Lukos had the bodies of at least half a dozen beggars and peddlers buried in the cellar of his house. But the other boys only laughed at this notion. It would be against the law, Julius argued, and even a magician would not dare violate the law. Julius' father was a judge, which was why he knew a lot about the law and such matters.

Oddly enough, the boys had never seen Lukos. For some reason the soothsayer seemed never to leave his house. One day, during the breakfast recess in school, Antonius had made the bold statement that Lukos never left because he had no legs. This had annoyed Publius, who was fond of contradicting anyhow, and he had objected: "Then he would have himself carried by his slaves." Whereupon Antonius replied:

"He has no slaves."

That had infuriated Publius. "What silliness!" he cried. "Lukos is rich. A consul who was visiting us once said Lukos made millions on his soothsaying. All the big shots go running to him because they can make a lot of money on his prophecies. They pay him plenty. The consul says he has even guessed the Emperor's secret plans. The Emperor doesn't know about it, but the senators and consuls do. It's just stupid to say Lukos has no slaves when every millionaire has at least a hundred. Why, we've got two hundred slaves."

"We've got a lot more," Antonius promptly retorted. "We've got two slaves for our goldfish alone. But Lukos has no slaves. My father told me so, and he knows better than your consul. Have you ever seen a slave coming out of Lukos' house? Have you?"

"No, come to think of it—that's funny," Publius admitted sheepishly.

"You see!" Antonius triumphed. "No slaves ever come out because there aren't any."

Flavius, who had been listening attentively, asked, "But who brings him his food?"

"Nobody," Antonius answered readily. "If he gets hungry, he produces a meal for himself by magic."

That was too much for Mucius. "Ridiculous," he snorted. "You can't make food by magic. Lukos probably goes out to eat every night."

"Without legs?" Caius exclaimed in astonishment. Whereupon they had all burst into laughter.

This conversation had taken place several weeks ago. At the moment the boys were feeling much less gay. And now Antonius had made them feel rather nervous with his silly idea that Xantippus might have been murdered.

Mucius frowned sternly at Antonius. "What made you think Lukos might want to murder Xantippus?"

"Oh, that's easy," Antonius was eager to explain. "Lukos is mad as anything at the school because we always make such a racket. That bothers him when he's trying to soothsay."

"That wouldn't be a good enough reason for him to murder Xantippus," Julius protested.

"He hasn't murdered him either," Antonius said. "He's just bewitched him and changed him into a pig, which amounts to the same thing."

The others laughed. And Julius remarked: "If Xantippus had been changed into a pig we'd hear him grunting in the next room."

"He was changed into a deaf and dumb pig," Antonius promptly replied.

"There aren't any deaf and dumb pigs," Julius disagreed.

They began arguing about whether or not deaf and dumb pigs existed. Publius, who took an interest in this problem, abandoned his sleeping position on the bench. As he sat up, he happened to glance at the wall behind Xantippus' desk. "Why," he exclaimed, "the writing tablet is gone."

At first the boys did not understand. Then they

realized he meant the tablet on which Rufus had written *"Caius is a Dumbbell."* What could have happened to it?

Mucius suggested that Xantippus had probably thrown it away out of annoyance. Julius thought otherwise. "He must have saved it to show to Rufus' mother as proof that Rufus was to blame for the fight with Caius."

"That's right," Antonius agreed. "A mathematician like Xantippus never does anything without good proof."

"Poor Rufus." Flavius sighed, and for a while the boys fell silent. Meanwhile it had grown lighter outside, but the sun had not yet risen, and Broad Street was still deserted.

"Let's go home. There's no sense sitting around here," Publius grumbled.

"Quiet!" Mucius whispered sharply. "I thought I heard something from the other room." He tilted his head and listened tensely. "There! Do you hear that?"

From Xantippus' apartment came a muffled groan. The boys stared in horror at the curtain.

3

A Bump of Considerable Diameter

"Should we go in?" Julius asked softly.

Flavius protested, stammering with fright: "Hadn't we better call the police?"

The others looked inquiringly at Mucius. On tiptoe, Mucius approached the curtain. He paused in front of it and listened again. The noise had stopped.

"Maybe it was only the wind," he said.

"I never heard the wind groan like that," Publius murmured. "Besides, there isn't any wind right now."

Mucius pulled himself together. "Bring your lantern over here, Antonius!" he ordered. "I'll see what's the matter."

Antonius brought the lantern. With one decisive movement, Mucius jerked the curtain aside. "Oh!" he breathed in amazement, and stood rooted to the spot.

The others peered over his shoulders. There was only a tiny window in Xantippus' room, but in spite of the dim light the boys instantly saw that something bad had happened. Almost all the furniture had been knocked over, and scattered around the entire room were rolls of papyrus, pictures, files, writing tablets, and articles of clothing. Only the bed and a large wardrobe in the corner were still upright.

There was no sign of Xantippus at all. His bed was empty, the sheets ripped.

The boys were so amazed by it all that they forgot about the strange noise. Cautiously, Mucius made his way through the litter of things on the floor. He stopped in the middle of the room and looked around, shaking his head in puzzlement. "Crazy!" he murmured.

The others followed him. Flavius, hanging back close to the entrance, ready to flee, asked anxiously, "But where is Xantippus?"

Antonius flashed his lantern into the tiny alcove which served as a kitchen. "Not here," he reported. Then he looked under the bed, but Xantippus was not there either.

"Where can he possibly be?" Flavius wondered.

"He's skipped out," Publius said, grinning.

"Yes, that's it," Antonius exclaimed. "He's sailed back to Greece because he's sick and tired of us. He had a fit of temper and knocked over all the furniture before he left."

Publius laughed scornfully. "I thought Lukos had turned him into a pig."

Just then the muffled groan was heard once more. This time it was louder and lasted longer. It came unmistakably from the corner where the wardrobe stood.

The boys froze in their tracks.

"There's something in there," Mucius whispered.

"A ghost," Antonius breathed.

"Let's get out of here," Flavius murmured.

But the others stared hypnotized at the wardrobe. The groaning began again, and then there was a hoarse croaking.

"There's someone locked in there," Mucius said excitedly. He started to creep toward the wardrobe.

"Don't open it!" Flavius warned in a choked voice.

"Yes," Mucius said, "we have to. He might suffocate."

"It isn't a person," Antonius insisted. "It's a ghost. A ghost can't suffocate."

"Shut up!" Mucius snapped. "Ghosts don't sit in wardrobes in the morning. I'm going to open it. Give me some light."

Antonius directed the glow of his lantern at the wardrobe door, but his hand was trembling and the feeble light danced like a will-o'-the-wisp up and down the wall. More croaking issued from the wardrobe. The key was sticking in the lock on the outside. Mucius boldly turned it, wrenched the door open, and stood back in amazement.

In the wardrobe sat Xantippus, tied up like a bundle of old rags. His hands were bound behind his back and a crude gag made of strips of sheeting had been wound around his face, leaving only his eyes and his unkempt hair visible.

"Xantippus!" the boys cried out.

From under the gag there came an irritable croak.

"Why is he sitting in the wardrobe?" Flavius said.

Xantippus produced a gobbling sound like a goose.

"He wants to get out," Antonius observed.

Mucius suddenly came to life. "Don't stand around like dumbbells!" he shouted at the others. "We can't leave him in there like this. Come on, help me! Give a hand!"

Xantippus was tightly wedged into the wardrobe, but by pulling together they managed to pry him loose. He fell roughly to the floor, growling furiously. Mucius unwound the gag, bent over their teacher and asked with concern: "How do you feel?"

Instead of replying, Xantippus closed his eyes and heaved a sigh.

"He's dying," Antonius said.

At that Xantippus opened his eyes again and growled ferociously: "By Jupiter and all the heavenly gods! Why did you wait so long? I almost suffocated. Quick, untie me! My arms and legs are dead. You'd better get a knife from the kitchen."

Antonius and Publius managed to untie the ropes around Xantippus' legs. With the big bread knife that Flavius brought from the kitchen, Mucius freed their teacher's hands. Xantippus moved his arms cautiously and began clenching and unclenching his fists, groaning softly. "Help me!" he ordered the boys. "I can't stand up."

The boys raised him to his feet and led him to his bed, where he sank down, exhausted. After a while he began feeling his right leg, his features twisted with pain. "My leg!" he complained. "I am certain I have sprained it. Of course, it's swollen. Oh—ouch! I can't possibly stand on it." Then his hands flew to his head and he exclaimed: "A bump! I thought so. And what a bump! The swelling is approximately round and of considerable diameter." He reached up to the shelf above his bed for a small polished metal mirror and stared gloomily into it for a long while. Mucius cleared his throat and ventured a respectful question: "How did you come to be in the wardrobe, sir?"

Xantippus gave the boys a long, mournful look. "I was assaulted last night," he said with a sigh.

4

The Mathematical Burglar

"Assaulted?" the boys echoed.

"Who did it?" Julius wanted to know.

"Did they want to kill you?" Antonius burst out enthusiastically.

"Quiet, please!" Xantippus croaked. He was still hoarse. "I don't know who the criminal was. I was in bed, sound asleep. In the middle of the night I was awakened by the sound of someone moving about next door in the classroom. 'Who's there?' I called, but there was no answer. I jumped out of bed and went to see what was the matter. That was foolish of me—I should first have struck a light, for it was pitch dark. Suddenly a pair of arms seized me. I tried to grip the unknown by the throat, but he was stronger than I and threw me to the floor. As I tried to get to my feet, I received a severe blow on the head and lost consciousness."

"Boy, oh boy!" Antonius breathed.

Xantippus threw him a stern look and continued: "When I came to, I was sitting in the wardrobe, bound and gagged. I heard the burglar rummaging among my things for a long time, as though he were desperately looking for something in particular. Finally he went away and all was quiet. It seemed ages before I heard you boys arrive. But I could not call to you because of the cloth over my mouth. If you had not freed me so soon, I would certainly have suffocated in that wardrobe."

Anxiously, he touched the lump on his head again, then felt his injured leg, groaning. "The whole affair is a mystery to me," he said. "Who would want to steal anything from me?"

"Perhaps a thief . . . ?" ventured Julius.

"I'm not rich, like Croesus. Besides, what money I have I keep in the bank. Still, you never know. . . . Clean up all this mess, boys. Then we shall see whether anything is missing."

The boys plunged into a flurry of activity. They picked up the furniture and books, dragged tables and chairs and chests back to their proper places. From his bed Xantippus directed the work. As they arranged each book, file, or picture they had to call out what it was, and Xantippus scratched notes with a stylus on a writing tablet. Finally they gathered up the scattered writing tablets and returned them to the chest which the burglar had turned upside down.

When all was restored to order, Xantippus sat staring thoughtfully at his list. At last he announced with astonishment that several mathematical textbooks and a few unimportant pictures were missing. "Odd," he said, shaking his head. "These things would have no value at all to a stranger." And with a sigh he added, "But for me they are a severe loss. My good old Pythagoras is gone. And the second roll of Euclid's mathematical writings. And my own monumental work on the acute angles of obtuse triangles . . ." His voice faded and he looked at his pupils with eyes full of distress.

Antonius seemed to understand his sorrow and offered consolation. "The burglar who did this may be studying mathematics and doesn't have the money to buy books. He heard that you were a famous mathematician and so he came here and hit you on the head. . . ."

But Xantippus told him to be quiet, and Publius sneered, "I never heard of a burglar studying mathematics."

Flavius had something on his mind. "Shall we call the police?" he asked timidly.

Xantippus would not hear of that. "Keep the police out of this, please. I know those boys. Just let one of those fellows stick his nose in here and I'll really be in trouble. I know how they work. Questions and more questions till I'm worn thin as a sheet of papyrus. They'll poke around among my things all day long, turn everything topsy-turvy and find all kinds of clues—only they won't find the thief."

"Yes, they're awful dumb," Antonius chimed in. "I once asked a policeman at the Forum how late it was. He stared blankly at the big sundial back of the rostrum and finally said, 'I don't know.' It was raining, you see."

"You talk too much," their teacher commented. "Your tongue will be your undoing one of these days."

Alarmed, Antonius squinted at the tip of his tongue.

"You may go now," Xantippus said. The recent experience had not sweetened his temper. Still, he felt it proper to add, "I am thankful to you for coming to my rescue."

"We only did our duty," Mucius said modestly. And Antonius, not in the least abashed by his teacher's sharp words about his tongue, put in innocently, "We didn't know you were in the wardrobe. We thought you had been changed into a pig. The way

Odysseus' men were—by the beautiful enchantress Circe."

Xantippus glared blackly at him.

"All right, get to your seats!" Mucius ordered, and started driving his friends out of the room. But Xantippus had other ideas. "There will be no school today. You may go home now. You need not come tomorrow either. I shall give the class a few days' vacation. I must stay in bed until my leg is better. I shall send word when school starts again."

The boys whooped with joy at the unexpected vacation. But Mucius suddenly became grave. Hesitantly, he asked: "Then . . . then you will not be going to see Rufus' mother today?"

Xantippus, who was now standing on one leg and straightening out his bedclothes, pivoted around. "See whom?" he asked absently.

"Rufus' mother. You were going to see her today because of what Rufus did . . ." Mucius paused and looked distressed.

Xantippus cleared his throat. "Oh yes—hm," he murmured. "Wait a moment!" Groaning, he crawled back into bed, pulled up the covers and lay back on the pillows, sighing with relief. For a while he stroked his beard reflectively. Then he said: "I had no real intention of going to see his mother. My idea was to give Rufus a good scare and teach him a lesson."

"Then Rufus can come back to school after the vacation?" Mucius asked happily.

"He may," Xantippus replied graciously. "On the whole he is not a bad pupil. I wouldn't want to make him miserable because of a single prank. I know what it means to a young Roman to be a pupil in the Xanthos School. And I hope you know it, too."

"Oh yes!" the boys cried sincerely. They really were proud of their school.

Xantippus nodded with satisfaction, but suddenly turned stern. He barked: "But woe betide you if I ever again see such bad conduct and unspeakable lack of discipline as yesterday's! If I ever do, you will all be expelled. And now, out with you!"

"This holiday is a gift of the gods," Julius said when they were out on the street. He rubbed his hands in glee. "We have to celebrate."

"Let's play cops and robbers," Antonius suggested. "I'm the robber and you can be the policeman. Or we'll play war. I'm the Roman and you're the barbarians. We can play chariot racing, too. I'm the driver and you're the horses . . ."

"You be a jackass and we're going to tan your

hide," Publius joked. "I have a better idea. Let's go down to the Tiber. A big Egyptian galley has moored at the cattle market. We can sneak on board and have a good look."

"That's dangerous," Flavius warned them. "If the sailors catch us they'll give us a beating. Let's play ball on the Field of Mars."

"No, I have another idea," Julius said. "A shipment of wild animals has come in at the Taurus Amphitheater. We can watch them being taken to their cages."

"Marvelous!" Antonius agreed. "There'll be elephants and lions and dragons. Come on!" He was about to start off at a run, but Mucius held him back. "We must go to see Rufus first," he said.

"Why?" the others wailed in disappointment.

"To tell him that Xantippus has called the whole thing off. Poor Rufus thinks he's been expelled. He expects Xantippus to come to see his mother. We can't leave him to worry all day long. That would be a mean trick."

"You're right," Julius said. "And then he can come with us."

They raced down Broad Street past the Capitol to the Forum. The sun had not yet risen, but a few clouds in the sky were flushed with pink, and the eastern horizon was quite bright. The Forum Romanum, which would be swarming with people later, was still almost empty. Only the innumerable pigeons were up and about, circling in huge flocks over the square, and a few slaves with shopping baskets were passing through on their way to the nearby markets, or returning with similar baskets heavily laden.

The boys crossed the Forum, turned into a narrow, dirty alley, and then climbed a steep stone staircase which led to the plateau of the Esquiline Hill. They were panting by the time they reached the top. Now they were in Minerva Square. From here it was only a short distance to Rufus' home.

Minerva Square was a quiet, open space surrounded by extensive pine woods where wealthy patricians had their mansions. In the center of the square stood the temple of Minerva, a plain, whitewashed building whose only impressive feature was the columns at the entrance, and three broad marble steps. But the little temple was very sacred because it was dedicated to the Emperor. Opposite the temple, in the shade of tall cypresses, was the home of Senator Vinicius, Caius' father.

"I wish I knew why Caius didn't come to school today," Flavius said, staring at the house.

"He'll say he had an upset stomach," Publius prophesied.

"Shall we tell him there won't be any school for a while?" Julius asked.

"No," Mucius decided fiercely. "Let him wait. Give him time to do his homework. It won't harm him. Come along!"

They hurried on past the house. Just as they reached the temple the sun rose, bathing them in golden light. Publius stopped suddenly. "By all the good gods!" he said in quiet horror, pointing at the temple.

On the whitewashed wall, angrily scrawled in blood-red paint, were the words:

CAIUS IS A DUMBBELL

5

Claudia

"Rufus did that!" Julius exclaimed.

"He must have gone off his head," said Publius. "If Caius' father sees it, there will be trouble!"

The boys threw anxious glances at the senator's house. Vinicius took the worship of the gods very seriously, and was a great admirer of the Emperor. It was common knowledge that he had donated a great deal of money for the building of the temple of Minerva.

"Is it bad to deface a temple?" Flavius asked.

"Is it bad?" Publius replied. "You can get in real trouble that way."

Antonius went up to the temple wall and dabbed his finger at the C of CAIUS. "I wonder where Rufus got the nice red paint," he said with admiration.

Mucius pushed him aside and tried wiping off the writing with the hem of his toga. But the paint was already dry. "Too bad," he said. "This scribble has to be erased."

"Maybe we can rub it off with a stone," Julius suggested. He looked around, but there were no stones in sight. The ground in front of the temple was kept extremely neat and clean.

"Let's use our styluses," Antonius said. But it was too late; two men were walking quickly toward the temple. Flavius instantly snatched up his school equipment and fled. Toga streaming behind him, he ran across the square and hid behind a dense hedge of oleander shrubs at the edge of the woods. The others did not hesitate for long and followed his example.

"Why did you run?" Antonius asked, panting.

"Those men might think we did it," Flavius replied.

"Quiet!" Mucius whispered sharply. "They can hear us."

The boys peered through the branches and saw the men disappearing back of the temple. One of them called out, laughing: "Take a look at that, Clodius. Somebody has written 'Caius is a dumbbell' on the temple wall."

The other man did not seem to see the joke. "Scandalous!" he growled. "An outrageous crime. Nothing to laugh at."

"Well, now, take it easy," the first man could be heard saying. "You can see it's a child's handwriting. Some silly kid's trick, that's all. You and I were young once, my dear Clodius."

"No," protested the man addressed as Clodius. "Young or not, I would have known enough not to desecrate a temple."

The two men emerged from behind the building and walked toward the stone staircase which led to the narrow alley. They were two elderly citizens in snow-white togas. One of them was a big, tall man; the other was short and spindly. The large man waved his arms in excitement and anger as he talked. Abruptly he stood still, grasped the short, thin man by the toga and shouted: "And I tell you, that isn't just a schoolboy prank. The temple is dedicated to the Emperor. This is an act of criminal blasphemy. The boy ought to have both hands cut off. Both hands! And that would be far too mild a punishment."

The thin man looked uncomfortable. "Yes, yes, you're right," he said, trying to pacify the other. "But it's none of our affair. We must get to our shops. We have a great deal to do today."

They moved on and started down the steps. First their legs vanished, then their hips and finally their heads. For a moment the bald head of the big man

CAIUS
iS A DUMBBELL

glistened in the morning sunlight; then it, too, dis-appeared.

The boys looked at one another in consternation.

"Do you hear that?" Antonius said. "He wants to have Rufus' hands chopped off."

"I told you it would lead to trouble," Publius said self-importantly.

"But nobody knows that Rufus did it," Flavius said.

"No matter, we have to get rid of that writing," Mucius said. He started pushing through the shrubbery, but Antonius held him back, whispering: "Somebody else is coming." He pointed toward the home of Senator Vinicius.

Adjoining the left wing of the villa was a high garden wall overgrown with wild grapevines. Where wall and house met there was a tiny door which, the boys saw, was now slowly opening. A small girl thrust her head out and looked in all directions.

"Claudia!" Mucius said in surprise. "What is she doing?"

Claudia was Caius' younger sister, and well liked by his classmates. She was gay and friendly and not a bit stuck-up. The boys used to let her play with them, but recently she had passed her eleventh birthday, which spelled the end of her carefree childhood. All at once she had been put under the care of several Greek governesses who trained her and taught her and did not allow her to leave the house unaccompanied.

But now Claudia slipped out and made straight

across the square to the shrubs where the boys were hiding.

"Don't run away, I have something to tell you," she called out as she ran. She pushed aside the branches and faced the boys.

"I saw you through the window. Something awful has happened. Where is Rufus?"

"Home," Mucius said.

"Oh, that's good." Claudia sounded greatly relieved. "He had better keep out of sight. My father knows all about it." She looked hot from her run, and her deep-blue eyes were glowing with excitement. Usually Claudia was elegantly dressed, and her hair was done up with the greatest care, but this morning she had slipped quickly into a plain tunic, and her long brown curls were tied carelessly with a narrow ribbon. She wore house sandals which probably belonged to her mother, for they were much too large for her.

"What does your father know?" Mucius asked sharply, his eyes narrowing.

"I'll tell you all about it," Claudia replied. "But I'm afraid of being seen over here. I slipped away from my governesses."

"Come on!" Mucius said. He took her hand and drew her along deeper into the pine woods. When

they reached a pleasant, mossy clearing, he stopped. "Have a seat," he said politely, pointing to a low, flat rock.

Claudia sat down and the boys gathered around her.

"Does your father know that Rufus wrote on the temple wall?" Julius asked.

Claudia bobbed her head energetically.

"Tell us, tell us!" the boys chorused.

Flattered at being the center of attention, Claudia quickly patted her curls into place. "Our slaves discovered the writing when they came back from market this morning," she began. "They told the secretary, who ran to my father right away. My father was at breakfast. He put down his glass of wine, left his bread and cheese and rushed into the main hall to look out of the window. When he saw the writing, he was furious. 'This is an outrageous desecration of the temple!' he shouted. 'Who did it?' The secretary couldn't say, so my father got angrier still and threatened: 'I will have you put in chains!' The secretary threw himself down at my father's feet, saying: 'Mercy, Master! Perhaps your son Caius knows who it was. It must have been one of his schoolmates.' Oh, I could have killed him for saying that."

"The secretary is an idiot," Antonius declared.

"Yes," Claudia said. "I never could stand him. My father sent for old Herodus, Caius' tutor, and ordered him to go to school and fetch Caius. Old Herodus turned pale and said: 'Caius did not go to school today, Master.' 'Why not?' my father roared at him. Shaking, old Herodus also threw himself down at my father's feet. 'O Master, don't punish me,' he pleaded. 'I waked Caius early this morning, but he locked himself in his room and refused to open the door. I knocked several times. Finally he called out that there isn't any school today and that his teacher has gone on a journey.' "

"What a fib!" Flavius said.

"What did your father do then?" Julius wanted to know.

"He himself went to Caius' room and brought Caius back with him. Caius was still wearing his nightshirt, and he looked real scared. Father is very strict with him. He led Caius to the window, pointed out the writing on the temple, and asked: 'Who did that?' At first Caius just gaped, but suddenly he flared up and said: 'Rufus, the son of Praetonius.' "

"Shame, shame!" the boys cried out indignantly.

"What a traitor," Mucius said, frowning angrily.

"We must punish him," Julius said.

Folding his arms, Mucius stood pondering for a moment. Then he announced: "We shall exile Caius.

He won't be allowed to play with us, and none of us must talk to him."

"For me he does not exist!" Antonius declared.

"I won't speak to him either," Claudia said, blushing. She was obviously genuinely ashamed of her brother. "And I know he lied. Rufus is a nice boy. He wouldn't daub red paint on a holy temple. He gave me a beautiful ivory doll for my birthday."

"But Rufus did do it," Mucius said.

Claudia stared at him, her big eyes rounded in amazement.

"Caius insulted Rufus' father," Mucius explained, "and they had a fight. This all happened in school."

"Rufus wrote 'Caius is a dumbbell' on a writing tablet yesterday," Julius added.

"And hung the tablet on the wall," Flavius said.

"So then Xantippus threw him out of school," Publius finished the tale.

Claudia turned her head from one to the other with growing concern. "Threw him out of school!" she exclaimed. The boys knew she was very fond of Rufus, and Mucius hastened to reassure her. "It isn't so bad. Xantippus forgives him."

Claudia's face lit up. "That's good," she said. But immediately she looked troubled again. "My father is awfully angry," she murmured. "I came out here because I thought Rufus was with you. I wanted to warn him."

"About what?" Mucius asked.

"Well, it was this way," Claudia explained. "My father didn't believe Caius—that's why he sent for the two policemen who patrol the square at night. He pointed out the writing on the temple wall and asked whether they knew anything about it. They were dumbfounded. 'We saw nothing of the kind last night,' one of them said. 'How is that?' my father asked. 'There was nothing written on the wall,' the policeman replied. 'We were sitting right by that wall of the temple for quite a while. We always have a little snack at night, just some bread and a few figs and a sip or two of wine. It was bright moonlight; we would certainly have seen the writing if it had been there at that time.' 'When was that?' my father asked. 'Shortly before the fifth hour of the night,' the policeman said. 'Did you observe anybody near the temple?' my father asked. 'Nobody at all, sir,' the policeman answered. 'And then we left.' He asked whether he should report the defacing of the temple, but my father ordered him to say nothing about it. 'I'll look into this affair myself,' he said."

"Oh dear!" Flavius murmured.

"That sounds bad," Mucius said with a worried expression.

"And then what happened?" Julius asked.

"Then the two policemen went away," Claudia reported.

"Perhaps your father intends to punish Rufus himself," Flavius suggested.

Claudia shook her head regretfully. "No," she said, "he has another plan. After the policemen left he asked Caius: 'How do you know Rufus did it?' And Caius answered: 'We had a quarrel.' 'That's no proof,' my father said. But Caius insisted on it. 'It was so Rufus, because it's his handwriting. I know his handwriting,' he said. On hearing that, my father said, 'Aha! That's enough. If it is his handwriting, there can be no doubt that he did it. I shall go personally to the prefect of the city this noon and denounce Rufus for malicious desecration of a temple.' "

The boys were too shocked to speak. The prefect of the city was a man noted for his harsh and extreme sentences. He was a man who did not know the meaning of mercy.

"Do you think the prefect will do something terrible to Rufus?" Claudia asked unhappily.

Mucius nodded somberly. "He has passed a death sentence on people just for laughing when the Emperor and his retinue went by."

"But Rufus is only a boy," Claudia cried out.

"The prefect wouldn't have a young boy put to death."

"Why not?" Antonius said. "Many children have been put to death. I once saw some being executed. They were three boys no older than we are. They were loaded with heavy chains and thrown into the Tiber. They screamed and struggled in the water, and the soldiers laughed. I raced down to the river bank to try to save them, but by the time I got there they had already drowned."

Claudia stared aghast at him for a moment. Suddenly she jumped up and sobbed: "You are lying!" And off she ran, plunging blindly through the shrubbery. Hair streaming behind her, she raced across the square toward the garden wall. Halfway there she lost both sandals; she stooped quickly and picked them up, but instead of putting them on she continued running barefoot. She slipped through the open garden door and slammed it shut behind her.

"My, but she's in a hurry," Publius said.

Mucius gave Antonius an angry look. "You shouldn't have told her that story," he said.

Antonius was hurt. "But it's true," he said.

"Such stories aren't for girls," Publius said.

For a while they sat in silence, thinking. The rays of the morning sun streamed through the shrubbery; the sky was blue, birds chirped and a breeze rustled in the tops of the pines. From the Subura the low hum of awakening street life rose up to them.

"Rufus must flee," Mucius said suddenly.

"Where to?" Publius asked.

Mucius had thought up a plan.

"Listen!" he whispered excitedly. "We'll hide Rufus in our cave. Tonight we'll bring him slave clothes. He'll dress up in those and then we'll take him down to the river. I know a place where he can swim across without being seen by the guards on the bridge. He will have to travel by night and hide by day until he reaches our country place. I'll give him a letter to Sallus, our manager, asking him to take Rufus in as a slave—just pretending he's a slave, of course. Sallus will do it—he's a real friend of mine. I always help him with feeding the pigs and milking. The police will never look for Rufus out there in the country, and he can stay away until the whole affair blows over."

"A wonderful plan!" Julius said admiringly. And the others chimed in with praises of Mucius. But Mucius put an end to this quickly. "Come on," he said. "We must go see Rufus at once."

They took a shortcut through the woods to a rocky parapet up which they clambered to a quiet boulevard. Then they ran along a quiet, shady street until they came to a large, old-fashioned building with tiny window openings. This was General Praetonius' villa.

Mucius knocked on the door. It was opened by a white-bearded slave who recognized the boys at once. "How is it you boys are not in school?" he asked with a kindly smile.

"We have a few days off," Mucius answered. "Our teacher has injured his leg."

The old slave chuckled. "I suppose you're all heartbroken about that, eh?" he said, his eyes twinkling with merriment. "And what brings you here?"

"We'd like to see Rufus. We have something important to tell him."

"Hm," the old man said. "I think Rufus isn't feeling well. Leastways I haven't seen him yet this morning. But you look him up for yourselves. You know where his room is. Come in."

"Not feeling well?" Mucius asked uneasily.

The old slave shrugged. "Just a guess. At any rate, he did not feel like going to school today, or he would have been up long ago."

They stepped into the vestibule, took off their sandals, and went on into the dimly lit, modestly furnished central hall. They knew their way around the house, for Rufus' mother Livia was hospitable and encouraged the boys to come visiting. The boys liked her very much.

Rufus's room was small, dark, and windowless, lighted only by a transom over the door. Lifting the doorway curtain aside, the boys stepped in. Rufus, who was lying in bed, sat up in alarm.

"What's the matter?" he asked in confusion. He drew up the blanket, for he was wearing no nightshirt. Oddly, his hair was soaking wet, as though he had just ducked his head into a tub of water.

"What's up? Why are you looking so queer?" he asked his schoolmates.

"You must run away!" Mucius said.

Rufus paled. "Run away? Why . . . what for?" he stammered.

"Come now, you know," Publius said in a rather sour tone.

"I don't know anything," Rufus murmured weakly.

Antonius stepped toward him and whispered: "Your life is in danger. Because of what you wrote on the temple wall."

Rufus shook his head in sheer bewilderment. "I wrote something on a temple wall? Are you all off your heads? What was it? What temple wall?"

"Never mind lying!" Julius said severely. "You wrote 'Caius is a dumbbell' on the wall of the temple of Minerva. Didn't you realize that temple is dedicated to the Emperor?"

Rufus looked around at his friends in utter perplexity. Suddenly he began grinning. "You're just trying to play a trick on me. Haha, I won't bite."

"We didn't come here to joke," Mucius said angrily. "This business is much too serious. Hurry up, get dressed and come along."

At this Rufus lost his temper. "Let me alone!" he shouted. "I swear I never wrote anything on any temple wall. It must have been somebody else. And if you don't believe me, that's just too bad!"

6

Handwriting

The boys were taken aback. It had not occurred to them that Rufus might not be the culprit after all.

"Swear!" Mucius demanded.

"I swear!" Rufus repeated firmly, raising his right hand.

Mucius whirled around and fixed the others with suspicious eyes. "What about the rest of you?" he asked threateningly.

"It certainly wasn't me," Publius said angrily. "I've told Caius often enough to his face that he's a dumbbell—there was no need for me to write it on a wall."

"Perhaps one of Vinicius' slaves is responsible," Antonius suggested. "Caius might have played some trick on him like slipping nettles into his bed. To get even the slave wrote 'Caius is a dumbbell' on the temple wall."

"What slave in Rome is crazy enough to dese-crate a temple?" Julius pointed out.

"We're the dumbbells," Julius said slowly, squinting rather anxiously at Rufus. "Didn't Claudia tell us that Caius recognized Rufus' handwriting at once?"

"That's a lie!" Rufus protested. "How can it be my handwriting if I didn't do it?"

Mucius frowned. "But Caius seemed to think he knows your handwriting very well."

Rufus gave a forced laugh. "That's a good one. Caius is too dumb to recognize anybody's hand-writing. He can hardly read yet."

His friends did not laugh at this joke. They looked at him seriously. This put an end to Rufus' humor. He fell silent and began thinking. At last he sighed with relief. "I can prove that it is not my handwriting," he said triumphantly.

"How?" Mucius asked.

"Give me a writing tablet!" Rufus said. "I'll write 'Caius is a dumbbell' and then you'll see right away that that scrawl on the temple could not have been written by me."

This sounded simple enough, and the others agreed. Rufus took a stylus and tablet and prepared to scratch the words into the wax.

"But you must write just the way you always do," Julius warned him.

"And write it as big as you did last night in school," Mucius directed.

Rufus nodded. He sat hunched on his bed, tilting his head to one side as he wrote. He kept running the tip of his tongue nervously over his lips. Having completed his sample of handwriting, he handed the wax tablet to Mucius.

"There, that's how I write it!" he said with self-assurance.

The other boys crowded behind Mucius and peered at the tablet.

"Well?" Rufus asked uneasily. "Why don't you say something?"

"Hm," Mucius mumbled, rubbing his nose in embarrassment.

"It looks just like the writing on the wall of the temple," said Antonius, who had an excellent memory.

"No," Flavius disagreed. "It looks altogether different."

"To tell the truth, I no longer remember it," Mucius admitted.

"Neither do I," said Julius.

"We'll check up on that right away," Antonius

said, snatching the tablet from Mucius' hand. "I'll run over to the temple and compare the two handwritings."

"Wait, I'll go with you," Publius said. "Otherwise you'll be telling us crazy stories when you get back."

"A good idea," Mucius said. "But be careful that nobody catches you near the temple—especially with that tablet in your hands."

"You can depend on that," Antonius said, and sped out the door, followed by Publius.

An embarrassed silence fell in the little room. Rufus refused to look at his friends; he sat staring absently down at his toes, which were sticking out from under the blanket. After a while he asked hesitantly: "Haven't any of you been to school today?"

"By the gods!" Mucius exclaimed. "We almost forgot to tell you. Xantippus has forgiven you."

Rufus looked up, scarcely daring to believe what he had heard. "He has . . . has forgiven me?" he murmured. "Then he doesn't intend to talk to my mother?"

"No," Julius said. "He only wanted to give you a good scare."

Rufus sat numbed. "If I had only known that . . ." he whispered under his breath.

But the others paid no attention. Flavius said: "After the vacation you can come back to school."

"You see, we're all on vacation," Julius explained, and he launched into the story of the assault on Xantippus.

"But who could have attacked him?" Rufus asked wonderingly, when Julius had finished.

"That's the mystery," Mucius said. "And the funny part of it is that nothing was stolen but a few silly mathematics books and pictures." He then went on to tell Rufus about Claudia and her father's threats.

Rufus was shaken when he heard that the senator wanted to report him to the prefect of the city. "But I didn't have anything to do with it," he stammered.

"If you really didn't, we'll go to the senator and tell him so," Julius said consolingly. He felt sorry for Rufus. All the boys liked Rufus—he was a good sport, and always full of fun and good ideas for games.

They heard Antonius and Publius returning, and even before he reached the door Antonius called out: "The handwriting is just the same." He came running in, wax tablet in hand. "I was right. The writing on the wall looks exactly like the writing on this tablet."

"It's true," Publius seconded. "I'll bet a gold

piece against a single sesterce that Rufus wrote it."

"On my word of honor, I didn't write it!" Rufus cried out in anguish.

"You must have," Publius said.

"No!" Rufus asserted at the top of his voice. Suddenly his eyes widened and he said, as though he had found the answer and were frightened by it: "My handwriting has been forged!"

"What? How?" Mucius demanded.

"Somebody has copied my handwriting," Rufus announced.

"But why?" Flavius asked.

"So that people will think I did it," Rufus replied, staring into space with sadness, resignation, and fright in his eyes.

"Well," Julius murmured, "who do you think could have copied your handwriting?"

Rufus hesitated for just a moment. Then he said softly: "How should I know?"

"We are wasting valuable time," Mucius said angrily. "You must run away. We have already planned where to hide you."

"No, I won't," Rufus declared hotly. "If I run away people will feel certain that I did it. My own father and mother would believe it."

At this Mucius' patience gave out. "You're crazy!"

he accused Rufus. "Do you want to have your hands chopped off? Or be dumped into the Tiber?" He instantly regretted these harsh words, for Rufus cried out in despair:

"You think I'm lying! But I really did not do it." Then he turned toward the wall and drew the blanket up over his ears. The boys could hear his smothered sobbing.

Julius tried to soothe him. "We don't think you're lying. But it is very hard to copy anyone's handwriting. My father once told me that. The forger would have had to study your handwriting for a long time in order to learn how you wrote any letter."

Rufus sat up with a jerk. "The writing tablet!" he cried out. "The tablet I hung up on the classroom wall. 'Caius is a dumbbell' was written on that."

The others did not understand what he was getting at.

"You're talking in riddles like an oracle," Publius said.

"Perhaps the person who broke into school wanted to steal that tablet in order to copy my handwriting," Rufus said.

"But nothing was missing except some books and pictures," Julius pointed out.

Rufus looked dismayed. But Antonius began to

jump with excitement. "Hey!" he exploded. "The writing tablet *was* gone. Don't you remember? It was not hanging on the wall this morning."

Their faces all brightened. "We must go back to school at once," Mucius said. "If it was stolen, Rufus is right; that will prove once and for all that his handwriting was forged."

"How so?" Publius asked.

"How so, how so?" Mucius mocked his manner. "Because otherwise no burglar would bother to steal a writing tablet."

"You have something there," Publius admitted.

"Get dressed quickly and come with us," Mucius told Rufus.

But Rufus looked embarrassed. "No . . . I . . . ah . . . I've caught cold," he stammered. And he went into a coughing fit.

"On the whole it will be better for him to keep out of sight," Julius said.

"All right, stay here," Mucius said. "We'll be back soon."

The boys piled their school things in a corner and set out at once. As soon as they were gone, Rufus peered hastily under his bed. He sighed again with relief and leaned back against his pillow.

———

Xantippus was surprised when his pupils unexpectedly returned. He was sitting up in bed, reading, his right leg wrapped in wet cloths. In the apartment's tiny kitchen a Negro woman was busying herself with the cooking. Hearing the boys, she peered curiously around the corner of the room and then grinned cheerfully at them.

"Teacher sick, no school." She chuckled. "Poor man, bad pains, oh, oh!" She rolled her eyes to express her sympathy, then returned to her pots and pans.

"Why have you come back?" Xantippus asked crossly.

Mucius asked for Rufus' writing tablet.

"What tablet?" Xantippus wanted to know.

"The one that has 'Caius is a dumbbell' written on it."

Xantippus was instantly suspicious. "What do you want with it?" he asked.

"Rufus would like to have it back so that he can erase it," Mucius lied boldly. "He's ashamed about it."

The boys had decided on the way not to mention the desecration of the temple to their teacher, for fear that it would stir up his anger against Rufus all over again.

"So he's ashamed, is he?" Xantippus said with satisfaction. "About time. The tablet must be lying in the chest over there."

"Isn't it hanging in the classroom anymore?" Julius asked hypocritically. He only wanted to know why Xantippus had removed it.

"No," Xantippus said. "I don't care to have such things on exhibit on the walls of my school. I put it away in the chest last night—you boys must have noticed it when you cleaned up."

The boys rushed to the chest and went through it from top to bottom, but the writing tablet was not there.

"It's gone," Mucius reported, inwardly triumphant.

"Then you boys must have misplaced it," Xantippus scolded. "That's what comes of your careless way of doing things."

The boys searched all the shelves, and finally went through the entire classroom, but the writing tablet could not be found. Back at Xantippus' bedside, Mucius made his solemn announcement. "The thief who was here last night stole Rufus' writing tablet."

"A strange thing to steal," Xantippus said vexedly. "That tablet isn't worth a copper."

The boys bid Xantippus good-bye. But as they

were on the way out, Mucius noticed something shiny lying under the wardrobe. He stooped and fished it out. "Look what I've found," he said.

It was a short, wide gold chain with a flat disc of gold at one end, a hook at the other. Apparently the hook had been forced open and bent upward. Mucius brought the chain to Xantippus. "Is this yours?" he asked.

"No," Xantippus replied. For a while he regarded the chain thoughtfully. Suddenly he gave a short laugh. "But I can tell you to whom it belongs."

"Who?" the boys asked excitedly, half guessing the answer.

"It belongs to the burglar," Xantippus said.

7

The Newspaper

"I remember now how it happened," Xantippus continued. "I tried to grip the burglar by the throat, but instead my hands closed on something metallic which came loose. That must have been the chain. Probably it was kicked under the wardrobe in our tussle." He examined the chain more closely. "This is the type of chain which goes on the collar of a rain cloak, as a sort of clasp. Look, here: the disc was sewed on to the collar. A few threads of wool are still clinging to the holes. There was probably a second disc with an eye for the hook. When I tugged at the chain, the hook was bent straight and slipped out of the eye. The chain is very beautifully worked, by the way."

"What are those funny pictures?" Antonius asked, rubbing his finger over the gold disc.

"Your hands need washing," Xantippus reproved him. "Those marks engraved on the disc are hieroglyphs—Egyptian picture-writing."

"Now all we need to do is find the owner of the chain and we'll have the burglar," Mucius said hopefully.

"Ridiculous," Xantippus said. "Rome has a population of half a million. A fine chance you have of finding the one cloak this chain belongs to. No, it's not much of a clue. Here, keep the chain; it's yours."

Delighted, Mucius thanked his teacher and dropped the chain into his pocket. The servant came in with a stack of damp cloths to apply to Xantippus' sore leg, and the boys were sent away. As they crossed the Forum, they passed by the great sundial back of the orator's platform and saw that the third hour of the day had already begun.

"We ought to hurry," Julius said. "Rufus must be terribly anxious for us to get back."

"Rufus can wait," Mucius said. "We must see Vinicius first."

"Why Vinicius?" the others asked in surprise.

"To keep him from going to the prefect," Mucius explained. "We'll tell him that somebody forged Rufus' handwriting."

"But he knows we're Rufus' friends and so he won't believe us," Publius objected.

This remark had a dampening effect on the boys' spirits. "Uhm," Mucius murmured. "I never thought of that."

"How about this?" Julius proposed. "We will take the writing tablet on which Rufus wrote for us this morning, and have my father look it over and compare it with the writing on the temple. Since my father is a judge, he will be able to tell right off that the writing was forged, and he can write a letter about it to Vinicius."

"How long will all that take?" Mucius asked.

"A couple of days," Julius said with a crestfallen air.

"That long?" Mucius exclaimed.

"My father is in Pompei right now," Julius explained. "He had to go down and preside over a gladiatorial show he sponsored."

"We cannot wait that long," Mucius said.

"Vinicius was once a judge himself," Flavius said. "Perhaps *he* can compare the handwritings."

"A fine idea," Mucius approved, and Flavius grinned proudly. Publius was sent off to obtain the writing tablet from Rufus, after which he would meet the others in front of Vinicius' house. Publius was the fastest runner among the boys; he had long, skinny legs and always came out first in races. Pleased with his assignment, he shot off like an arrow.

In the meanwhile the Forum, empty a few hours ago, had become a bustling place, swarming with people who poured in from all the side streets. From the noise and buzz of talk, it might have been a chariot race at the Circus Maximus. Everywhere there were groups of citizens discussing the affairs of the day, their togas billowing in the breeze.

An especially large crowd stood in front of the massive building which housed the national archives. Curious, the boys forced their way boldly to the front of this crowd. But they were disappointed. There was nothing to see except the daily newspaper, which had just been hung out by two of the Censor's officials. The latest news had been written on it in neat hand-writing, and the people were pressing forward eager-ly to read. In the front row of the crowd stood several well-dressed slaves, the copyists of rich patricians, who copied the news on wax tablets with astonishing speed. Back at home their masters waited impa-tiently for the transcribed bulletins.

Antonius, Flavius and Julius wanted to go on; they had been hoping for something more sensa-tional than the dull old newspaper. But Mucius did not move and stared in fascination at the news. "There's something about the temple of Minerva here," he whispered to the others.

"Where?" Flavius asked.

"Not so loud!" Mucius shushed him. "There. Down near the middle."

The writing was small, and it took Antonius, Julius and Flavius a moment before they discovered the item. Then with growing alarm they read:

Last night the Temple of Minerva on the Esquiline, erected in honor of our Emperor, was desecrated by the impudent hand of a shameless boy. Smeared with red paint on the eastern wall of the temple are the words *"Caius is a Dumbbell."* This impious act will certainly arouse the indignation of all right-minded citizens of Rome. It is high time that the authorities took energetic measures to combat such delinquency among our modern youth. The temple faces the home of His Honor, Senator Vinicius. In all likelihood the insult is directed against the senator's son Caius. Young Vinicius is a pupil at the well-known Xanthos School. It seems evident that the guilty boy would be one of his fellow pupils with whom Caius may have quarreled. We hope that the senator will promptly question his son in order to discover the culprit and turn him over to the police at once. Public opinion will not rest until this young hooligan is behind bars.

A Respecter of the Emperor

8

Senator Vinicius

The boys looked around nervously, but fortunately nobody was paying attention to them.

"If they recognize us as Xanthos' pupils they'll tear us to pieces," Antonius said tensely.

Flavius turned white and tried to make himself as small as possible.

"Follow me quietly," Mucius whispered. With deliberate slowness he sauntered toward the marble staircase. Whistling idly, he climbed the steps between the columns. The others followed his example, but as soon as they reached the top they dashed off in a wild flight down the length of the corridor, leaped down the steps three at a time, and gave the Forum a wide berth. Not until they reached the foot of the Esquiline Hill did they begin to feel fairly safe and slow their pace.

"Did you notice the slaves copying the news?" Publius said. "Before long all Rome will know that Caius is a dumbbell."

"Perhaps Vinicius' copyist was there, too," Flavius worried.

"No doubt about it," Mucius exclaimed. "We must get to Vinicius before he does." And he started running again.

In front of Vinicius' villa Publius was waiting for them.

"You're a regular marathon runner," Mucius said in praise.

"Oh, I practically walked," Publius said, still panting.

"What did Rufus say when you told him his writing tablet had been stolen from school?" Julius asked.

"Nothing," Publius replied. "He was sound asleep. I didn't bother to wake him, just took the tablet and scooted."

Mucius pulled a bronze ring, and a big, uniformed doorkeeper who looked like a former gladiator opened the front door. "What do you want?" he asked gruffly.

"We must speak to the senator," Mucius said.

The doorkeeper raised his eyebrows in astonishment. "And who do you think you are?" he demanded.

"Pupils of the Xanthos School," Mucius answered.

The doorkeeper was not impressed. "Oho, isn't that wonderful!" he said. "The master will be flattered, I'm sure. Is he expecting you?"

"That isn't necessary," Mucius said. "He knows us. We've come about Rufus."

"Rufus? Who is Rufus?"

"Rufus is our friend—the son of Marcus Praetonius," Mucius replied with dignity.

The doorkeeper frowned in thought. "Marcus Praetonius?—Marcus Praetonius . . . Oh yes . . . isn't he the general who lost the battle against the Gauls?"

"That isn't Rufus' fault," Mucius said indignantly.

"Go away, you kids!" the doorkeeper snorted. He was about to slam the door in their faces when Claudia, accompanied by one of her governesses, appeared at the back of the vestibule. Mucius instantly shouted, "Claudia, Claudia! He won't let us in."

Claudia came running up and ordered the doorkeeper to admit the boys. "They're my friends," she said firmly.

The man's manner instantly changed. He flung open the door with a flourish, calling out: "Right foot forward, please!" to ward off the misfortune it would bring upon the household if anyone entered with his left foot foremost.

"How nice of you to come," Claudia said joyfully. "I was awfully bored."

She was dressed now in a flamingo pink tunic, with a flower-embroidered hem. On her feet were dainty little silken house sandals.

"I'm sorry we have no time to play," Mucius said gravely. "We must speak to your father at once. We've found out for sure that Rufus didn't do it."

"Oh, that's wonderful!" Claudia said, clapping her hands with pleasure. "Take off your sandals and come along."

The boys quickly slipped out of their sandals, shot a triumphant glance back at the doorkeeper and ran along behind Claudia. She led them into a large courtyard, surrounded with columns, and instructed them to wait. "I'll tell my father you want to see him," she said. She slipped through a curtained opening at the farther end of the court.

The boys straightened out the folds of their togas and gave each other a critical inspection to make sure that they looked respectable enough for the senator. Flavius went to the fountain in the center of the court, moistened his hands and slicked down his hair. The others followed his example.

"Hello!" a voice suddenly spoke behind them. They whirled around and saw Caius standing between two pillars, a rather sheepish smile on his face. "What are you fellows doing here?" he asked with forced cheerfulness.

Their only response was a hostile stare.

Caius gave them a sickly grin. "Forgotten how to talk?" he asked. But the boys remained stubbornly silent. At that his face flushed and he hissed furiously: "Idiots!" Then he shrugged, turned on his heel and went out.

"Now he knows we're mad at him," Flavius remarked.

"We'll settle with him yet," Mucius growled.

"Just wait till we get him to our cave," Antonius said. He dipped his right foot into the basin of the fountain, but immediately jerked it out again. "Whew, is that cold!"

The curtain parted, Claudia appeared and called excitedly, "Come along, my father is waiting for you."

The boys followed her. She led them into a lofty, magnificently furnished room. The floor was covered by deep carpets, and wide couches with plump cushions stood about everywhere. There were paintings on the walls, and from the ceiling hung costly lamps of Alexandrian glass. Claudia pointed to a tall double door between two marble statues. "My father is in there, in the gymnasium," she said.

"Is he in a good mood?" Antonius asked.

"Not very," Claudia said, wrinkling her nose. "I only talked to him through the door, but he sounded like a bear. Are you scared?"

"Not a bit," Mucius snapped, but he cast a rather worried glance at the door.

"Go right in," Claudia said. "He won't bite. He knows you, after all." She sat down on a couch, leaned back gracefully against the cushions and smiled encouragement at the boys.

Mucius gave a quick tug to his toga once more, and opened the door.

The senator was lying on a wide marble table, having his back massaged by two slaves. The room smelled strongly of perfumed oils. He turned his head toward the boys and asked harshly: "Well, what do you want?" His hair was snow white, his eyebrows very bushy and still a dense black, which looked odd to the boys. His words came out in staccato rhythm because the slaves were at the moment pounding his back with their palms.

"We've come about Rufus," Mucius said.

The senator glared at them. "If you've come to tell me a pack of lies, you can get out right now!" he said threateningly.

A rotten beginning, Mucius thought. But he tried to go on. "You see, we are Rufus' friends—we go to school with him . . ."

"I know that," the senator interrupted. "Why hasn't Rufus come with you?"

"He's sick, caught a cold," Mucius replied.

"Nonsense," Vinicius growled. "He's hiding because he has a guilty conscience."

"He honestly did not do it," Mucius hastily went on. "We would put our hands in the fire for him."

The senator sat up, pushing the slaves aside. "Vouch for him all you like," he said. "You won't get anywhere with me that way." He took his tunic from the slaves, put it on, and in spite of his considerable girth swung nimbly off the table. Stooping, he picked up a bundle of wax tablets and held them under Mucius' nose. "Here, take a look at the newspaper. My copyist has just brought me the latest edition. All Rome knows about the desecration of the temple. People expect me to find the culprit and turn him over to the police. I intend to go directly to the prefect of the city now and lodge a charge against Rufus. His vile act is an insult to our dearly beloved Emperor, and he must pay for it. I am sorry, but consideration for my friend Praetonius cannot be allowed to sway my decision."

Mucius was alarmed to hear that the newspaper report had already reached the senator. So they had come too late. "But Rufus has sworn he did not do it," he stammered in confusion.

That was as far as he could get. "Then he lied," the senator rapped out. "My son says it is Rufus' handwriting. My son would not tell an untruth."

"Rufus' handwriting was forged!" Mucius cried out.

The senator was taken aback. "What's that you say?" he asked.

"His handwriting was forged," Mucius repeated. "We have definite proof of it." And he told Vinicius about the theft of the writing tablet from Xantippus. "Someone stole it in order to have Rufus' handwriting to imitate," he finished his tale.

At this point Julius spoke up. With a self-important expression he said: "Here is Rufus' real handwriting." And he handed Vinicius the tablet Publius had just brought.

Vinicius glared at it. "Why, here it is again: Caius is a dumbbell!" he exclaimed angrily.

The boys were frightened; they had not expected this reaction.

"That . . . that's our fault," Mucius stammered. "I mean, we had Rufus write the same thing again because we wanted to compare his writing with the scrawl on the temple."

"Hmm," Vinicius growled. But he sounded somewhat appeased. "And who would you say forged Rufus' handwriting?"

"That we don't know," Mucius admitted.

"It certainly wasn't any of us," Flavius protested, flushing.

Vinicius turned to Mucius again. "You say Rufus wrote this?" he asked, pointing to the tablet.

"Yes," Mucius said. "We thought that with your experience as a judge you would see at once that the writing on the temple wall was a fake."

"I don't know much about handwritings," the senator said, but the theory evidently intrigued him. Stepping to the window, he stood there for a while looking alternately at the writing tablet and the inscription on the wall of the temple. Finally he said: "These two handwritings certainly look very similar."

"They would have to be similar if someone were deliberately making a copy," Publius said, grinning.

Vinicius returned to them. He planted himself in front of the boys and looked at them searchingly. "All right," he finally said. "I will look into this theory of yours." He turned to a well-dressed slave who had been lingering respectfully in the background throughout the conversation. "Sulpicius, run and see whether Scribonus is at home. Ask him to come to me at once. If he is already at the Apollo Library, take an express sedan chair and bring him here."

The slave hurried out. Vinicius sat down, and asked the boys to be seated also. "Scribonus is director of the Apollo Library," he said. "He is the outstanding handwriting expert in Rome. If Scribonus attests that the writing is forged, it is forged. And if he says it is genuine, it is."

"It is forged," Mucius said with conviction.

"That is for Scribonus to say," the senator held.

"What will you do if it is forged?" Flavius asked.

"That I don't know," Vinicius replied, laughing. "But at any rate we will know that Rufus is not guilty. He would not be likely to forge his own handwriting, would he?"

"Of course not!" the boys burst out. They were feeling a great deal better. Vinicius wasn't so unreasonable after all. In fact he became quite friendly; he asked them about their parents, about school, and about what they were planning to be.

"I want to be an orator," Julius said. "My father takes me to the Senate with him so that I'll learn."

"And I'm going to be a charioteer," Antonius said at the top of his voice. "What a thrill, flying around the arena with four fry Arabian stallions harnessed to the chariot. The people will throw flowers down upon me and the Emperor will crown me with laurels . . ."

Their pleasant chat was interrupted by voices

behind the door. In a moment Sulpicius entered, followed by a tiny old man with a long gray beard: Scribonus. The boys realized at once that he must be a Greek. Almost all the scholars in Rome were Greeks; moreover, Romans did not wear beards. Scribonus wore no toga, only a shabby tunic which badly needed laundering. But although the man looked like a beggar, the senator greeted him with great respect. "How kind of you to come," he said, and started to explain what he wanted.

Scribonus listened attentively, head tilted to one side. "Louder!" he said impatiently every so often. Finally he took the writing tablet, held it close to his eyes and asked irritably: "Caius is a dumbbell? Who is this Caius?"

Vinicius' good humor evaporated; he frowned with annoyance. "Caius is my son," he snapped.

"So I thought," Scribonus said, unperturbed. He thrust a finger into his ear and wiggled it back and forth. Then he handed down his verdict: "This was written by a boy about twelve years old. The writing is crude, but already has personal character. And where is the supposed forgery?"

"Over there on the temple wall," Vinicius said, pointing out of the window.

Scribonus walked to the window, but took hardly a glance at the temple. "That's much too far for me," he decided. "I'm nearsighted. We will have to go over there."

Vinicius and Scribonus went out, followed by the boys. As they passed through the main hall, Claudia sprang from the couch and joined the party. "What did my father say?" she asked Mucius in a low voice.

"He's been most cooperative." Mucius replied, rather condescendingly.

They went out through the front door and crossed the short distance to the temple of Minerva. Scribonus again examined the writing tablet. Then he went up close to the wall, so that the tip of his nose was almost touching the stone and stood in silence for a long time studying the painted red letters. At last he said: "The paint has run into the center of the U, and the upper part of the A is also smeared. But these details do not deceive me."

The boys were holding their breath. But Scribonus took his time. From his tunic he took out a large, multicolored handkerchief, rubbed his nose deliberately, replaced the handkerchief, and stood looking again from wall to writing tablet. Finally he spoke. "The writing on the wall is by the same hand as the writing on the tablet."

9

Wet Clothes and Empty Money-Box

Vinicius, who had been so reasonable, was angry once more. "Bring that Rufus to me at once!" he growled. "I'll talk to him." He thanked Scribonus for his professional services, took Claudia by the hand, and returned to the house. Scribonus handed the writing tablet to Julius and strolled off. The boys angrily watched him go.

"He would mess things up for us," Publius said.

"So Rufus lied after all," Mucius murmured. "Yet I would have sworn he was telling the truth."

"What's the use now," Julius said. "The die is cast and Scribonus has ruined our case. It looks bad for Rufus."

"He can still run away," Flavius said.

"It's too late for that now," Mucius said. "And he doesn't want to, anyway. We'd better go and get him."

This time they were not in such a great hurry.

Their footsteps lagged, and it took them nearly fifteen minutes to reach Praetonius' house.

The old, white-bearded slave looked pale and troubled as he opened the door for them. "The gods be thanked you have come," he exclaimed. "My mistress has asked about you several times. Go in quickly. Something terrible has happened."

Each of the boys felt a sinking sensation in the pit of his stomach. They were so flustered that they forgot to remove their sandals. They made for the main hall, and hesitated uneasily at the entrance. Rays of sunlight fell through the roof-opening upon the household altar in the corner, which was adorned with early spring flowers. A cat lay asleep on a couch. The first impression was one of peace and harmony. But then they saw Rufus' mother, Livia, sitting motionless in an armchair close by the wall from which her husband's weapon collection hung. She was in tears, and her favorite slave girls stood around her in dismay. When Livia caught sight of the boys she sprang to her feet, and came toward them.

"Rufus has been arrested," she said, struggling to steady her voice.

The boys were speechless with horror.

"You must help me!" Livia pleaded. "You are all his friends, aren't you? You know he has done nothing bad. They say he is guilty of desecrating a temple. I cannot believe that—my son is no hoodlum. About half an hour ago an army officer and two soldiers came to take him to prison. Rufus was in his room, but he must have heard us talking about him, because he came out wrapped only in his blanket and asked, 'What's the matter, Mother?' The officer put a hand on his shoulder and said, 'You have insulted our Emperor. You are under arrest.' Rufus wrenched away and came running to me, crying, 'I swear I did not do it, Mother.' He was as white as this tunic of mine. He wanted to say more, but the officer shouted at him to be quiet, and even threatened him with his sword. They led him away just as he was, without even giving him a chance to get dressed. I was nearly out of my mind—I would have run after them, but my girls held me back for fear I would be arrested, too. My poor boy," she sobbed, "it can't, it can't be true."

The boys looked down at the floor in embarrassment. At last Mucius murmured, "We did not believe it either."

Livia gave him a look of gratitude. "They tell me that you were here earlier, shortly before Rufus was arrested. Why was Rufus not in school? What has been going on?"

Mucius told her the story, with the other boys

filling in his omissions. Livia listened, more and more astonished. "Rufus behaved very foolishly in school," she said sadly. "But Caius also did wrong. He knows how much Rufus thinks of his father. Ever since the news of this unfortunate battle arrived, Rufus has been a changed boy. He is upset about his father, so that his anger at Caius was only natural. But angry or not, he is still not the kind of boy to desecrate a temple. There are plenty of other walls to write on in Minerva Square. There is one point I do not understand," Livia said. "You told me that the senator wants to see Rufus. Has Senator Vinicius already called on the prefect of the city or has he not?"

"No," Mucius said proudly. "We stopped him from doing that."

"And yet somebody must have accused Rufus," Livia said. "Don't you see?"

Here was a startling thought. If the senator had not yet filed charges against Rufus, who was responsible for the arrest? "We are the only ones who know it is Rufus' handwriting," Julius said thoughtfully. "I mean, just us and the senator and Claudia and Caius."

"And Scribonus," Mucius said. "But no—Rufus was already arrested by the time Scribonus heard the story."

"Perhaps Caius denounced him," Publius suggested.

"Impossible!" the others exclaimed.

"Why not?" Publius asked. "Caius was pretty mad."

"That's silly," Julius pointed out. "Caius knew his father was going to file charges against Rufus. Even supposing he wanted Rufus punished, he couldn't have planned it any better—his father, the famous senator, going to the prefect personally. Besides, the prefect would never arrest someone just on Caius' say-so."

This last point convinced the others.

"Perhaps it was Vinicius' secretary, or old Herodus, Caius' tutor," Flavius said. "They also knew about Rufus."

Julius had an answer for that, too. "They are slaves," he pointed out, "and slaves cannot bear witness against a Roman citizen. Besides, they would never have dared to act without their master's knowledge."

"But it must have been someone," Mucius exclaimed, baffled.

"Simple enough—someone saw him doing it," Publius said calmly.

"Saw whom doing it?" Julius asked, desperately making signs to Publius to keep quiet. But Publius did not understand. "Someone saw Rufus writing 'Caius is a dumbbell' on the temple wall."

Livia looked at them in fright. "So you do believe that Rufus is guilty?" she asked anxiously.

Publius looked down at the floor, and the other boys also avoided meeting Livia's eyes.

"You cannot believe that," Livia said firmly. "My son swore that he did not do it, and he has never lied to me." But her confidence was wavering, for she turned to one of her slave girls and asked, "When did Rufus come home last night?"

"I don't know," the girl said. "But Rompus must know, Mistress."

"Did Rompus bring Rufus home from school last night?" Livia asked the boys.

"Rufus had already left," Mucius said. "Rompus hurried home, hoping to meet Rufus on the way."

"I have not spoken to Rompus about this," Livia said. "Unfortunately he is not here now. I was unwell this morning, and Rompus was sent to the doctor to fetch healing herbs for me. The doctor lives on the other side of the Tiber River, so that Rompus will not be back for three hours at least. We can only wait for him. Perhaps you will be kind enough to come back later. I need your help; I myself can do little about this. Of course I have already sent an express courier to my husband, but the man will take at least five days to reach Gaul, assuming that he can find enough changes of horses along the way. Ten days there and back at best—and meanwhile what terrible things may happen. We must find the real culprit as soon as possible, and you can help me. You won't desert Rufus, will you?"

The boys assented heartily, but they were secretly wondering in what way they could help Livia, for by now they were almost certain that Rufus was guilty. Livia, however, clung to a last hope. "Rufus could not have come home late last night," she said. "Otherwise Rompus would have told me."

The boys did not understand.

"You told me that the desecration of the temple could have taken place only between the fifth and the sixth hours of the night, didn't you?" she asked.

"Yes," Julius said. "The policemen swore that they saw nothing before the fifth hour, and by the time we discovered the writing in the morning the paint was already dry. Which means it had to have been put on the wall not much later than the fifth hour of the night."

"That would mean that Rufus would have had to leave the house last night," Livia continued. "And that is impossible. The door is locked and well guarded; he could not crawl through the windows because they are much too small; and the garden wall is too high to climb over."

Once again the boys were taken aback. From their own experience they knew there was no chance of getting out of their own houses unnoticed late at night.

"Perhaps Rompus secretly let him out," Julius suggested.

"No," Livia said firmly, "that is out of the question. I trust Rompus completely. He is utterly loyal to us—we could not have a better tutor for Rufus. Rompus is more a member of the family than a slave. My husband brought him back from Macedonia when he was still a boy, and we have raised him as if he were our own son. In fact we intend to give him his freedom soon, and he will then be able to choose whether to stay with us or open a small shop somewhere in town." She sighed. "I suppose it is best for you all to go home now. There is nothing we can do at the moment. We must wait to hear what Rompus has to say."

"We left our school things in Rufus' room. May we get them?" Julius asked.

Livia nodded. The boys hurried to Rufus' room, followed by Livia who held the curtain aside for them so that they would have more light. The boys picked up their stuff and started to leave, but Mucius suddenly remembered his lantern which Rufus had taken by mistake the night before. He looked around for it.

Rufus' room was furnished with Spartan simplicity. Along one wall stood the bed, over which hung a portrait of Rufus' father in full general's uniform. Along the other wall was a small table, a hassock, and a shelf for schoolbooks and toys. He had no wardrobe; his clothes hung from big nails.

"What are you looking for?" Julius asked.

"My lantern," Mucius said. "Rufus took it with him last night by mistake. It was an expensive lantern and has my name engraved on it. My family will make a fuss if they notice that I don't have it."

"It ought to be around," Antonius said, peering about the room.

"What is it?" Livia asked, coming in.

"I'm looking for my lantern," Mucius said, flushing. "I . . . I lent it to Rufus . . . and I'd like to have it back."

"It must be among his things on the shelf," Livia said.

Mucius rummaged, but found nothing on the shelf except Rufus' books and writing materials, eleven marbles, a top, several broken wooden soldiers, a small knife, a fragment of Alexandrian glass, and a money-box for savings.

Publius took the money-box from his hand and shook it curiously. "It's empty," he said, replacing it on the shelf.

Meanwhile Antonius had crawled under the bed. He emerged with a bundle of clothing. "This is all I could find," he said in disappointment.

But Livia was startled. "It's most unlike Rufus to hide things under his bed," she said. "He is usually so orderly." She took the clothes from Antonius and promptly exclaimed: "Why, these clothes are soaking wet."

She held them up to show the boys. The clothes looked as though they had just been taken out of a tub full of water; she had only to press them for fat drops to splatter down upon the stone floor.

"Why should they be wet?" Livia said in wonderment.

At this moment a slave girl came rushing into the room. "Rompus is already back, Mistress!" she said breathlessly.

"Already?" Livia asked. "Then he could not have gone to the doctor."

"No, Mistress," the girl said. "He turned back to bring you important news."

10

The Hole in the Wall

As Livia and the boys came back to the hall, Rompus, a handsome young man, came joyfully toward them, with the words:

"I bring good news, Mistress!"

"Tell me!" Livia asked eagerly, and it was evident from her expression that she was thinking of Rufus.

"Our master has won a great victory," Rompus reported. "The latest edition of the newspaper was hung out just as I was crossing the Forum. Our master has defeated the rebellious Gauls, and there is great rejoicing in the city."

The boys were delighted, and the slave girls crowded around Livia, congratulating her. "Now everything will be well, Mistress!" one of them said.

"Rufus will be released immediately," Mucius said happily.

"Rufus released?" Rompus asked. In the excitement no one had told him about Rufus' arrest.

"I fear not," Livia said to Mucius, and he realized that she would rather have had news about Rufus than about her husband's victory. She started to say something more, then reconsidered and sent the slave girls out. Rompus alone was permitted to remain. She sat down, beckoned the boys to gather around her, and said in a low voice: "The Emperor is jealous of my husband, who is adored by his troops. You know that the Emperor insists on being worshiped as a god, and he will not stand for any rival gods. The prefect of the city is ambitious and is now more likely than ever to mete out harsh punishment to Rufus as a way of pleasing the Emperor."

The boys nodded intelligently. It was an honor to be told such political secrets, but there was a certain amount of risk in it, too. It was extremely dangerous to make any slighting remarks about the Emperor. Flavius looked anxiously around to make sure that no one was eavesdropping.

Rompus could contain himself no longer. "What has happened to Rufus, Mistress?" he burst out.

"Rufus is in prison," Livia said.

Rompus paled. "In prison!" he breathed, horrified.

Livia told him what had happened. Then she

asked sternly, "Where was Rufus last night? Why are his clothes soaking wet?"

Rompus fell to his knees before her, stammering, "Oh Mistress, it is all my fault! I should have stopped the boy . . ."

"So he was out after all!" Livia murmured. "Where did he go? How? When did he slip out?"

Rompus looked penitently at his mistress. "Rufus had already left school last night when I went to fetch him," he said. "These young gentlemen told me he had not felt well and had gone home."

"We only said that because we didn't want to tell on Rufus—about Xantippus, I mean," Flavius said.

"I hurried home," Rompus continued, "but Rufus was not back yet. He arrived half an hour later."

"Why did you fail to come and tell me?" Livia asked.

"You were ill, Mistress. There were strict orders not to disturb you," Rompus replied.

"But why did he come so late?" Livia asked.

"He would not explain, Mistress," Rompus said. "He looked very downcast, did not answer my questions, and went straight to his room. I was worried by this behavior and watched him through an opening in the curtain. I wondered why he did not take off his cloak, for his supper was standing ready for him. He took tinder and flint and lit his lantern. When he did so, I noticed that it was not his own."

"It was mine," Mucius put in.

"Then he emptied his money-box," Rompus continued, "pouring the money into a small bag. It occurred to me that he intended to run away, but I did not stop him immediately because I was curious to see how he would go about it. I decided it would be useful to learn his tricks, and so I hid myself. That was a piece of stupidity on my part; I should never have let him out of his room. He came out and sneaked through the hall into the garden. I followed close behind. In the garden he raced across the lawn toward the boxwood hedge, jumped over it, and suddenly disappeared. At that I really began to worry; I ran after him, but it was already too late. I was alarmed to find a hole in the wall that we never knew anything about because it is overgrown with ivy on the outside and concealed by the hedge on the inside. The hole was too small for me to squeeze through; all I could do was stick my head through and shout after him: 'Stop! Stop! Rufus, come back at once!' But he paid no attention to me and continued on into the woods. I had to run all the way through the house to the entrance and have Titus open the door for me. I lost so much time that

Rufus was out of sight before I started after him. I searched for hours, but could not find him anywhere."

"When did he return?" Livia asked.

"He was gone all night," Rompus replied guiltily.

"All night!" the boys and Livia exclaimed in one breath. "He only returned home this morning, shortly after sunrise," Rompus said.

"Where had he been?" Livia asked anxiously.

"He refused to tell me," Rompus replied. "He looked utterly worn out, was no longer wearing his cloak, and had not brought back his money or the lantern. What worried me most of all was that he was soaked to the skin. I insisted on his telling me where he had been, but he refused even to speak. Finally I threatened to go to you, Mistress, whereupon he became very excited, grasped my arms and cried out: 'If you do, my father will be lost!' "

"What in the world did he mean by that?" Livia asked.

"That I don't know, Mistress," Rompus replied. "But his despair seemed so genuine that I believed him. 'You must not betray me!' he pleaded. 'Nobody must know where I have been, not even my mother. It would bring misfortune upon us all.' He begged so hard that finally I gave him my word not to tell.

If I had only guessed these dreadful consequences, Mistress, I certainly would have gone to you. Perhaps we would have been able to save him. I could have helped him to escape in time; we could have gone to the country together and hidden." Rompus fell silent; he sat and stared woefully into space.

"It is too late for that now," Livia said. "I ought to be angry with you for neglecting your duty, but you acted in good faith. We must all work together now to help Rufus. But how many riddles there are! Above all I can't see how my husband can be involved in this thing. If only we could find out where Rufus was last night."

"We could visit Rufus in prison and ask him," Antonius proposed.

Rompus shook his head gloomily. "We would not be admitted," he said. "Besides, prisoners are strictly forbidden to talk."

"He must have been hiding out in Minerva Square," Publius said.

"It wouldn't take him all night to write 'Caius is a dumbbell' on the wall," Julius objected.

"And how do the lost cloak, the wet clothes, and the money fit in?" Mucius pondered.

"Maybe he used the money to buy red paint," Flavius suggested.

"Bosh," Mucius said. "After sundown there's not a shop open in all of Rome."

"Something tells me that Rufus fell in with evil companions last night," Livia remarked thoughtfully. "There is no other explanation for his behavior and for his staying away so long. Somebody forced him to write 'Caius is a dumbbell' on the sacred temple, perhaps with the intention of blackmailing my husband. Perhaps there are other political motives behind this business. If we had some proof that Rufus was forced to do it, the prefect would have to release him. We must try to find this blackmailer, or whatever he is."

"It seems to me that the man into whose hands Rufus fell must be the same person as the man who assaulted the teacher Xanthos," Rompus said. "These two incidents in a single night—there must be some connection."

"If only there were some way to find this scoundrel," Livia murmured. "But we haven't the slightest clue to go by."

"The chain!" Antonius suddenly shouted.

"What chain?" Mucius asked.

"The chain you have in your pocket. It belongs to the burglar, doesn't it?"

"Oh that," Mucius murmured. He took the chain

out of his pocket. Livia and Rompus examined it curiously.

"A valuable chain," Rompus said. "High oriental officers wear such chains on their cloaks."

"Perhaps the robber is a Persian general," Antonius said thoughtfully.

"More likely it was stolen from the cloak of a Persian general," Publius suggested.

"I'm afraid this chain is not much help," Livia said.

"I have an idea!" Mucius exclaimed.

"What is it?" the other boys asked.

"Lukos . . ." Mucius said, his voice lowered almost to a whisper.

"Lukos?"

"Yes," Mucius said. "He has second sight, after all. Let us go to him, show him the chain and have him say who it belongs to."

Antonius was overwhelmed. "Will that be exciting!"

Livia also thought the idea good. "This Lukos is supposed really to have second sight," she commented. "I've heard the most highly placed people say so."

But Julius, Publius, and Flavius maintained an embarrassed silence.

"Are you scared of him?" Mucius challenged.

"Go on!" Publius mumbled.

"Why should I be scared?" Julius said, scratching himself behind his ear.

"I'm not scared either," Flavius hastily put in.

11

Snakes

They met in Minerva Square two hours later. The weather had turned foul; it was very chilly, and dirty-gray rain clouds were scudding across the sky. Flavius' teeth were chattering. He had drawn the hood of his cloak far down over his ears. Perhaps his shivers were due as much to the thought of Lukos as to the cold.

Antonius showed them a small dagger he had concealed in the folds of his toga. "Just to be on the safe side," he remarked mysteriously. He then made a great show of hiding the weapon under his toga again.

"You act as though Lukos were dangerous," Julius said nervously.

"He might try to put a spell on us, after all," Antonius said.

"In that case your dagger won't be any help," Julius replied.

"A dagger always comes in handy," Antonius insisted. "Odysseus put out the Cyclops' eye with one."

"That was a sharpened stake," Julius said.

"We might take a stake along, then," Antonius offered. Mucius urged them to get moving. "We must be back home before the doors are locked for the night," he reminded them.

"Have you any money with you?" Julius asked.

"Why?" Mucius was taken aback.

"Lukos won't prophesy for nothing. I haven't a single copper with me."

Antonius and Publius were also penniless. Mucius was furious. "We should have thought of that before," he reproached the others. "All I have is my regular pocket money. Thirty-five sesterces. That's all I own."

"It'll cost more than that, but maybe we can owe him the rest," Flavius suggested.

"Or we can tell him to send the bill to Livia," Julius said.

"No," Mucius said. "Lukos won't use his second sight unless he sees money right under his nose. We can't waste time either because Rufus has to be rescued as soon as possible. Who knows what he may be going through right now."

"It's horrible in prison," Antonius said. "They

chain the prisoners up and give them only bread and water. Rats run over their faces, and they're beaten, too. I once passed by the prison and heard some awful screams."

"How much money do you fellows have at home?" Mucius asked firmly.

That was an embarrassing question.

"Not much," Publius murmured.

"I have a gold piece my uncle gave me for my birthday," Flavius admitted.

Pleased, Mucius patted him on the back. "Fine!" he said. "That's a hundred sesterces already. What about you?" he asked Julius.

"I've saved a little," Julius stammered. "I wanted to buy the *Collected Works of Julius Caesar*. They cost three hundred sesterces. I've saved up two hundred already."

"Then you'll have to donate a hundred of them," Mucius decided generously. Julius sighed in resignation.

"I can borrow something from our cook," Antonius said quickly. "We have a famous cook who comes from Gaul. My father paid a fortune for him."

"Run and get the money!" Mucius ordered them. "I'll wait here for you."

Flavius, Julius, and Publius returned in short order. Julius brought his hundred sesterces, Flavius his valuable gold piece, and Publius a heap of small copper coins. Antonius arrived a little while later, and with a long face. His cook had proved to be a disappointment. "What a skinflint!" he complained. "He wouldn't give me anything at all. Says he doesn't have any money. But I fixed him." He held up a round cheese, broke it into pieces, and offered a piece to each of them.

"I don't want cheese, I want money," Mucius said.

"I have some money, too," Antonius replied. "I asked my father for an advance on my allowance. He happened to be home and was in a good mood on account of Praetonius' victory over the Gauls. 'Here's fifty sesterces for you,' he says as gracious as Jupiter in person. 'Buy yourself figs in honey!' You know what? For this money we could get a whole barrelful of figs."

"This money doesn't go on food," Mucius said, taking the coins. He gathered all their contributions and wrapped the coins in a clean handkerchief. "We now have two hundred and ninety-seven sesterces. That ought to be enough. After all, all he has to do is look at the chain and tell us who the burglar was. That should not cost too much."

They set off, and half an hour later turned into Broad Street. The closer they came to Lukos' house, the deeper grew the silence among them—like a patrol nearing enemy lines. When they reached the big door which they had often stared at with such curiosity, they stood indecisively for a while. Across the street was their school, and they regarded it almost with affection.

"I hope Xantippus doesn't see us," Flavius said.

"He's lying in bed and groaning over his leg," Publius said.

"Don't you think we ought to do something about getting in?" Julius proposed.

Mucius nodded agreement. "I'll knock," he said, and began drumming his forefinger against the door. When nothing happened, he knocked again. Still nothing stirred, and Publius began pounding his fist against the door. Finally Julius and Antonius took part, kicking vigorously with their sandals against the thick wood. When all this had no effect, Mucius tried the latch—and the door opened. It had not been locked at all. A few feet beyond it, however, was another door; this was bound with strips of iron and had neither lock nor latch. Halfway up the door was a square pane of yellow glass, and the boys peered curiously through. Each in turn staggered back in terror. Behind the pane of glass a frightful, grimacing face, illuminated by a greenish light, was staring at them.

"That's Lukos!" Flavius gasped.

They waited anxiously for a while, but nothing stirred. Finally Mucius peered through the glass once more and said, "It isn't Lukos. It's only a mask."

"What a horrible mug," Julius said. "What's the idea?"

"It's supposed to scare away evil spirits," Antonius said.

"It could scare away even the good ones," Publius grumbled.

"Here's a ring beside the door," Antonius noticed. "It must be there for a reason."

"Pull on it," Mucius suggested.

When Antonius pulled the ring there sounded from somewhere deep inside the building a quivering bell-tone, like a sigh from the world of shades.

"What a gruesome noise," Julius murmured.

Suddenly the door flew open without a sound, as though moved by ghostly hands. The boys stared, but there was no one in sight.

"He opened it by magic," Antonius whispered.

Before them stretched a long, dark corridor. Back of the yellow pane of glass in the door hung a wooden box, to which the mask was fixed; it was lighted by a small oil lamp with a green shade.

"Clever, that," Julius whispered.

"What do we do now?" Publius asked.

"We'd best stay here at the door," Flavius recommended.

"I see a curtain back there," Mucius said. They walked slowly down the corridor as far as the curtain and then hesitated in front of it. There was a faint moldy smell.

"Well, what are you waiting for?" a hoarse, unfriendly voice called out abruptly. "Come in."

The boys started in fright, but automatically obeyed. Mucius pushed the curtain aside and went right in; the others followed him uneasily. They found themselves in a large, vaulted room only dimly illuminated by a flickering fire in a fireplace. The bare walls glistened damply and were completely windowless. All around stood high columns, their tops lost in deep shadows. From each column hung a grinning mask as ugly as the one behind the front door, and all the masks were illuminated from within so that they looked like so many horrid ghosts.

The soothsayer sat behind a large table with his back to the fireplace, and stared at the boys in silence. He looked even eerier than they had imagined him. Long, dirty-yellow hair fell in tangled strands down to his shoulders and over his forehead as far as his eyes, and his face was strangely painted. The upper part of it was white; from his mouth down

it was painted black, so that the top of his face seemed to be detached from his body. He wore a long black cloak embroidered with silver stars, and in his left hand he held a ball of polished metal which reflected the glow of the fire.

"Come closer," Lukos said, hoarsely lisping.

The boys edged up to the table, which was heaped with writing tablets, and yellowed parchments. Their eyes fell on a sharp short sword which filled them with distrust. But they were disturbed most by a basket filled with writhing snakes. Lukos scrutinized the boys with small, cunning eyes which seemed to them somehow full of hatred. "What do you want?" he asked.

Mucius hastily thrust the chain into Julius' hand. "You talk better than the rest of us," he whispered. "You speak to him."

Taken by surprise, Julius laid the chain on the table. He kept a respectful distance from the snakes. "Good day," he said politely. "We hoped you could tell us who this chain belongs to. There was a burglary at the home of our teacher Xantippus, and we would like to know who the burglar is because Rufus has been arrested. You see, we are Rufus' friends, but he is innocent and that is why we have come to you. We have heard that you know everything, so perhaps you can help us."

Julius fell silent and gazed hopefully at Lukos. But his speech seemed to have made no impression. The soothsayer stared intently at the chain and did not say a word. The boys did not know whether he had gone into a trance or just fallen asleep with his eyes open.

Julius cleared his throat. "We have an idea the chain belongs to the burglar. So we would like to know what his name is and where he lives. That should not be a hard job for you, should it?"

Still Lukos did not reply. He closed his eyes and remained silent and unmoving. It was uncannily still in the room; the boys could hear nothing but the low crackling of the burning sticks of wood in the fireplace.

"Maybe he wants his money first," Publius whispered.

Julius summoned up his courage once more. "We will pay, of course," he said to Lukos. "What will it cost for you to use your second sight for us? We have money with us."

The effect of these words was startling. Lukos sprang to his feet—he was much taller than the boys had imagined, at least a head taller than Publius, who was lanky and big for his age. Pounding the metal ball on the table, the soothsayer thundered, "Get out!"

The boys were stunned.

"Get out of here, you shameless brats!" Lukos screeched. Suddenly his hand flashed into the basket and he threw the wriggling snakes at them.

The boys screamed with terror. They all ducked at once, and luckily the knot of snakes flew over their heads. A single snake became detached from the rest—it hit Flavius in the face, bounced off, and fell to the floor, where it wriggled right side up, raised its head and hissed at the boy. Flavius almost fainted with shock, but seeing his friends making their escape from the room, he uttered a piercing cry for help and flew after them. As if pursued by the Furies, they raced down the long corridor, squeezed through the two doors in a body, and ran down Broad Street almost all the way to the Forum. They did not stop until they reached a public fountain, where they greedily drank the cool, clear water flowing from the mouth of a stone lion. Gradually they grew calmer. Finally Julius said, panting, "I guess Lukos took a dislike to us."

"We escaped death by a hair," Antonius said.

"Magician or not, he has no right to throw snakes at people," Publius complained.

"They must have been poisonous," Antonius said, leaning over the edge of the fountain for another drink. But suddenly he straightened up with a cry of anguish. "Oh! Help! A snake has bitten me! Help!" He writhed and twisted convulsively, while the others stood helplessly around him. Suddenly something fell to the pavement with a ringing sound. It was the dagger he had hidden. During their wild flight it had slipped down under his toga, and as he stooped over, it had pricked him in the stomach.

Publius and Julius roared with laughter. Antonius, too, was enormously relieved and able to appreciate the joke. Flavius alone remained silent. He could still feel the horror of the damp, cold, slimy snake on his face.

"Where is Mucius anyway?" Publius asked, looking around in surprise.

There was no sign of Mucius. It was already dark, and the streets were almost deserted. A gust of wind whipped up a billow of dust in front of them. Thunder boomed in the distance.

"I don't understand that," Julius said uneasily. "Where can he be?"

"Probably he ran first, before we did, and went right on home," Publius said.

"That isn't like him," said Julius. "He's never been the first to run away. And besides, he has our money with him."

"He thought maybe we would fool around and he wouldn't get home on time," Flavius said. "His father is very strict with him about that."

This seemed convincing, but the others still felt queer about Mucius' absence. However, they did not have time to think much more about it. A brilliant streak of lightning flashed across the sky, followed by ear-splitting thunder. Immediately afterward a fearful shower of hail began pounding down upon them.

"We'd better get home!" Publius shouted. He tucked up his toga and began running with great leaps down the street. The others followed him at top speed.

12

A River inside a Building?

Mucius had not separated from the others because he was in a hurry to get home. He had not even run away when they had. He stayed with Lukos. For he had made an astonishing discovery.

After handing the chain to Julius, he had gone to the rear of the group. Standing there, more or less inconspicuous, he had taken the opportunity to look around the place. He was curious to find out how Lukos had made the ironbound door open without himself leaving the vaulted room. Close to the floor, along the wall, Mucius discovered several cords. *Aha*, he thought, *that's the trick*. Then his eyes fell on a woolen cloak lying half-hidden behind a pillar near the fireplace. He was startled, for the cloak seemed familiar to him. While Julius was talking he stole over to it, lifted it, and examined it closely. Sure enough, it was Rufus' cloak. On the left shoulder was the neatly mended tear which Mucius had seen before. Here was clear proof that Rufus must have visited Lukos. But why? And why had he left his cloak behind?

Puzzling over this, he paid no attention to the way the interview was going. Then suddenly he heard Lukos' shout and saw his friends fleeing wildly. He hesitated for a moment, and that was his mistake, for by the time he began running after them, he was several yards behind. He raced into the corridor and found the inner door with the secret mechanism already shut. The others must have slammed it as they rushed out. He shook it, pounded his fists against it; but his friends did not hear.

This was a pretty mess. He was caught like a mouse in a trap. It was so dark that he could not even see the walls of the passageway. The only light was the greenish sheen from the mask behind the pane of yellow glass. He looked at his hands and saw that they were shaking, and found, to his surprise, that he still was clutching Rufus' cloak. He was scared; his heart was pounding so loud he thought he could hear it.

Ridiculous, he told himself. *He won't do anything to me.* But he was afraid of Lukos. Should he ask the soothsayer to let him out? He tiptoed back to the curtain and peered through it. Lukos was going around with a basket, picking up something.

He moved in a peculiarly awkward fashion, and every step he took sounded as though he were pounding a block of wood against the floor. Stooping seemed hard for him, too, for he groaned aloud each time he bent his back.

With a shudder, Mucius saw that the floor of the room was crawling with snakes. He backed into the corridor. As he groped along the walls, he felt a ladder under his hands. Quickly, he put on Rufus' cloak and lifted his foot to the lowest rung. It was a long climb before his head bumped against something hard. He felt what was above him and realized that it was a ceiling trapdoor. When he braced himself against the ladder and pushed, it opened upward. Drops of rain pelted into his face; it was thundering and lightning, but this did not drive him back. He swung up onto the roof, quickly closed the trapdoor, and sat down upon it. Then he sighed with relief. He was out of that dreadful place. For a while he sat there feeling quite pleased with himself, but gradually he began to be uncomfortable. He could not very well sit out here on the roof all night long in the pouring rain, with the lightning flashing all around him. *Maybe I can jump off,* he thought. Luckily the roof did not have a sharp pitch. He crawled on hands and knees to the edge and waited for a flash of lightning. Then he looked down, and with a shudder started back. The building was far too high for him to venture a jump; he would break every bone in his body.

Now he crawled along the edge of the roof, hoping to find a rain gutter on which he might shinny down. But this hope failed; there were no gutters. He made himself as small as he could, hunched up against the driving rain, and stared despairingly into the darkness. But suddenly he sat bolt upright. By the latest lightning flash he had caught a glimpse of the flat roof of another house, almost within reach. The distance between the two roofs was hardly longer than the length of his arm. Immediately, he crawled down to the edge and prepared to jump. At the next lightning flash he leaped, fell forward on his face— but he was safe. He would certainly find another trapdoor on this roof, and he made up his mind to rouse the people who lived in the house and ask them to let him out. They would be strangers, but they certainly could not be as bad as Lukos. But how could he account for the fact that he was stranded on their roof? "I'll simply tell them the truth," he decided.

Cautiously, he crawled forward. But suddenly his hands reached out into empty space; he lost his balance and fell headfirst into space. *It's all over,* was his last thought. *The fall will kill me.* Then he dropped with a loud splash into water and sank like a stone.

Mucius was a good swimmer, and with a few vigorous strokes he brought himself quickly to the surface. It was pitch dark; he could see nothing at all. Water had got into his nose, and his head rang as though a thousand pins were sticking into his brain. Rufus' cloak felt as heavy as iron on his back, and he had to keep treading water vigorously to stay on the surface. He had not the faintest idea where he could be. He must have fallen into a river, for he could feel a strong current under his feet. But how was that possible? The Tiber was at least half a mile away from here, and there was no other river near. *Perhaps I am dead,* he thought in sudden terror. *Perhaps I am swimming in the River Styx which leads to Hades.* But that was really too fantastic. The dead were supposed to wait nicely on the shore until Charon took them across the Styx in his ferry. Besides, you didn't feel sick to your stomach when you were dead, and he certainly was feeling badly from all the water he had swallowed.

Suddenly he realized that it was no longer raining, although it had just been pouring cats and dogs, and that the wind had stopped completely also. But he still heard the rain beating down high above his head. He gazed upward and for a second, by a flash of lightning, caught sight of the sky framed in a square opening. No doubt about it—there was a roof above him with a skylight through which he must have fallen. He was inside the house next door. But then how could there be a river inside a house? How strange.

Growing tired of treading water, he let the current carry him along, and in a short time came up against a smooth wall. It felt like marble. Then he felt ground underfoot and realized with delight that the depth of the water was rapidly dropping. Soon it reached only to his waist, and before long was gurgling harmlessly around his ankles. He waded along the wall, stumbled upon a flight of stone stairs, climbed up and sat down exhausted on the top step.

He felt altogether done in and so weary that he could not frame a single clear thought. If only he could figure out where he was. He cursed the darkness; because he could not see he did not dare move from his place, for fear of falling again. But suddenly he burst into laughter. In a flash he had realized where he was. He had fallen into the Baths of Diana—right into the swimming pool. What a joke! He knew these baths very well; they were an elegant place of recreation for rich patricians, and he had often been here with his father. He had never known that the building was located directly back of Lukos' house. How often he had happily swum in this very pool into which he had just fallen so unexpectedly.

At this point he realized what enormous luck he had had. The water of the Baths was drained out every night; that was the reason for the powerful current. If he had tumbled in here only a little later, he would have broken his neck on the marble floor of the pool.

He jumped to his feet and groped around until he found the front entrance. But the doors were firmly locked. And there was no other exit; that he knew. Here he was, locked in for the second time. And there was no help for it; he would have to wait all night, until he was let out. He was soaking wet, too—but at least he was not sitting on a roof in the rain.

He found a marble bench, folded Rufus' cloak into a pillow, stretched out, and fell asleep at once.

13

The Baths of Diana

Next morning he was rudely awakened. A brawny Arab was stooping over him, shaking him roughly by the shoulder. "This time I've caught you, you scamp," he railed. "This is the second time you've sneaked in here at night! Get up. You're going straight to the police."

Mucius started up, stammering, "What's the matter? Where am I? Who are you?"

"I am the superintendent," the Arab said. "How did you get in here?"

"I fell through by accident," Mucius said, pointing to the skylight high overhead through which a bit of morning sky could be seen.

"You're lying." The superintendent grunted. "You jumped in here night before last, too. Yesterday morning you got away from me, but you won't be so lucky today."

"I'm not lying," Mucius cried out. "I did fall in last night and never before."

"Oho, you deny it! What's your name?"

"Mucius Marius Domitius," Mucius said proudly.

"Ha!" the superintendent exclaimed with righteous wrath. "Then you're the one." And he thrust a bronze lantern under Mucius' nose. "So. Here's your name, right here: Mucius Marius Domitius! This is your lantern. That proves it. Lying won't do you any good."

Mucius was speechless. It actually was his lantern, the very one Rufus had taken by mistake.

The superintendent grinned triumphantly. "I found the lantern yesterday morning on the floor of the pool. You're a liar and deserve a good thrashing."

But Mucius was paying no attention, for a stirring thought had occurred to him. Could Rufus also have been in the Baths of Diana yesterday? "What was the boy like, the one you found here yesterday?" he asked quickly.

The superintendent was startled. "What's that? What was he like? Like you, of course."

"That couldn't be," Mucius said. "He can't have looked like me because I wasn't here."

The superintendent's bad temper returned. "So here we go again! Of all the bare-faced . . . Listen, you little scamp, you have some way of getting in and bathing without paying the entrance fee. For that kind of trick you'll go to prison."

This frightened Mucius. Prison was the last place he wanted to go. "I didn't intend to sneak in," he said. "I'll pay. What is the fee?"

"Ten sesterces, children half price," the superintendent said.

"I'll bring you the money today," Mucius said. "No, wait a minute, maybe I have it with me . . ." He hastily rolled up his toga, reached into the pocket of his tunic and found to his relief that he had not lost the handkerchief with the money. He untied the knot, picked out a silver coin worth twenty sesterces, and gave it to the superintendent.

"But I have no change," the superintendent said, his eyes riveted on the money in the handkerchief.

"No change required," Mucius said generously.

The superintendent hesitated. "Where did you get all that money?" he asked suspiciously.

"It's my pocket money," Mucius boldly claimed. He did not feel like telling the complicated story of how he happened to have the money with him.

"Your father must be awfully rich to be able to give you so much pocket money," the superintendent said slowly.

"My father is Marius Domitius, the Tribune," Mucius said.

The superintendent's eyes widened in disbelief. "What's that?" he exclaimed. "His Excellency Domitius? You mean it?"

Mucius gave a superior smile and pointed to the

lantern. "There it is!" he said. "Marius Domitius. You just read it to me!"

The superintendent's manner changed abruptly. He bowed low, stammering. "Excuse my words—I beg your pardon for them. Please don't report this little incident to your father. I did not realize—I let my temper run away with me. After all, I am in charge here and have to see that the rules are observed. We can't have just anybody sneaking in and using the baths without paying. Besides, it's dangerous. I drain the water out of the pool every night. If boys get into the habit of sneaking in via the roof, one of them sooner or later is going to jump into the empty pool and break his bones. And then won't I be in trouble? You were very lucky, young sir, that there was still enough water in the basin. Shall I dry your clothes? You can't go home in that state."

"No time for that," Mucius said, suddenly realizing that he had not been home all night. "How late is it anyway?"

"The sun has just about risen."

"I must hurry," Mucius said, and started at a trot for the entrance. Almost immediately, however, he slowed down to a stop. "Tell me about the boy who was here last night," he asked.

"When I opened the doors yesterday morning," the superintendent said, "a boy dashed out of the building, almost knocking me down as he went by. It happened so quickly that I only caught a glimpse of him from the back. I couldn't catch him either; he shot off like a barbarian. He must have come in by way of the roof the night before. That is the only way he could have got in, because I make sure the place is empty before I lock up every night, and this is the only entrance. When I found you on the bench this morning, I naturally thought you were the same fellow. But if you say you're not, you're not," he added in hasty apology. "You'd better take your money back."

"Never mind about that," Mucius called, and trotted off.

"Very kind of you, young sir," the superintendent called after him.

Mucius ran the short distance to Broad Street, crossed, and made a detour around the Forum. He did not want to be seen by people in his present condition—his clothes were wet and filthy and his hair an uncombed shock. But suddenly he stopped dead as though struck by a bolt from the blue. "Heavenly gods!" he murmured to himself. "Rufus is innocent." For it had suddenly occurred to him that Rufus could not possibly have written "Caius is a dumbbell" on the temple wall. Rufus had been locked up all night long in the Baths of Diana.

14

A Letter to the Emperor

When Mucius had finished his story, his friends gazed at him in silence. They did not know whether to be awed or to burst out laughing. What a wild tale—how were they to believe it? On the other hand there were the things he had brought back with him—Rufus' cloak, which was still wet, and his own lantern. Apparently he was not telling tales— in which case he was a hero and deserving of great respect.

They were in their secret cave, sitting on rickety boxes around a table on whose cracked marble top a candle was burning. Playing one day on the Esquiline Hill, they had come across this roomy cave in the rock, and had promptly appropriated it for their own use. It was their official headquarters. Here they met whenever they had anything important to discuss, and here they hid when it seemed wise to keep out of sight for a short while. One dark corner was piled with old junk which they had collected around town—and which they intended to use someday to furnish their cave. Over the entrance they had hung a tattered old rug to serve as a curtain.

Publius was the first to express his doubts of Mucius' tale. "You mean to tell us you spent the entire night locked up in the Baths of Diana?" he asked slowly.

"You can ask the superintendent if you don't believe me," Mucius replied, affronted.

"What did your folks say about your being out all night?" Flavius asked timidly.

"I was lucky," Mucius said. "They were at the theater yesterday afternoon, and afterwards they went to a party. So they came home late and slept late in the morning. Only our doorkeeper saw me this morning, and he won't tell on me."

"If I had known you were going to stay at Lukos', I would have stayed, too," Antonius said.

"I didn't stay by choice," Mucius said. "I was trapped there when you idiots slammed the door behind you."

"Would Lukos have done anything bad to you?" Flavius asked.

"That I can't say," Mucius replied, "but snakes were crawling all over the place, and I didn't like that."

"I would have stabbed Lukos with my dagger," Antonius boasted.

"If you hadn't fallen down dead from fright first," Publius mocked him.

"Quiet! All this is beside the point," Julius interrupted them. He pushed the candle aside, leaned across the table and looked searchingly into Mucius' face. "So your idea is that Rufus spent the fatal night locked up in the Baths of Diana, too?" he asked.

"I've explained the whole thing to you," Mucius said impatiently. "Rufus must have gone to see Lukos. Then he must have jumped into the Baths of Diana. In the morning when the superintendent opened the door he scooted out and ran away. And the only way he could have got in was the way I did, through the skylight in the ceiling. That must have been between the first and second hours of the night, when there was still enough water in the pool. If he'd jumped half an hour later, he would have broken his neck. So Rufus is innocent. He could not have written on the temple wall."

"But what made him visit Lukos?" Flavius asked.

"The gods alone know that," Mucius said. "All I know is that if he was inside the Baths of Diana, he could only have got there by crossing roofs from

Lukos' house. Lukos' house is the only one around that is as high as the Baths."

"What Mucius says makes sense," Julius said excitedly. "Remember Rufus' clothes that we found under his bed? They were soaking wet."

"So there," Mucius burst out, pleased by this support. "They were wet because he jumped into the pool at the Baths of Diana."

"We must do something at once," Julius said.

"But what?" Flavius asked.

"We'll go to see Livia and tell her all about it."

"What can Livia do?" Publius asked. "She herself said that she is powerless. The prefect of the city won't receive her because he knows that the Emperor is down on Praetonius."

"Then we have to go to the Emperor himself," Flavius reasoned. "If the Emperor orders Rufus' release, that's all there is to it."

That was a bold idea.

"What do you know!" Publius jeered. "Flavius is turning into a hero in his old age."

"That isn't a bad idea," Mucius said. "We can prove to the Emperor that Rufus is innocent."

"It's not as easy as all that," Julius said. He dropped his voice and went on in a whisper. "The Emperor is heavily guarded. He lives in fear that someone will try to kill him. You don't get admitted just like that—you have to ask for an audience, and that can take days."

"I know what we can do," Antonius said with a wild conspiratorial expression.

"What?" the others asked sulkily. Antonius' suggestions were apt to be pretty crazy.

"We'll write him a letter," Antonius rapped out. "He can't be scared of a letter."

The others were stunned. For once Antonius' proposal was sensible. They could leave the letter at the palace and it would surely be delivered to the Emperor at once.

"But who is going to write it?" Flavius asked.

"You, of course," Publius said. "You have the best handwriting in the class. For once it will come in handy."

Flavius protested, but was voted down.

"What shall I write on?" he complained.

"That's easy," Julius said, taking a parchment roll out from under his toga. "Here is a book of Cicero's orations. I don't like to part with it, but we'll use the back for the letter. It's fairly clean."

Flavius had objections. "A letter on the back of a book! What will the Emperor think! He's likely to read the book and not the letter."

"The Emperor is smarter than you are," Mucius

said firmly. "We can't take the time now to go looking for paper or wax tablets. This is an emergency. The Emperor will understand. Just cross out the writing of the book."

But Julius would not hear of that. "No, don't cross it out!" he pleaded. "That would be a pity, and besides the Emperor might be annoyed. He thinks the world of Cicero and so he'll be pleased to get the book. Go ahead and write on the back—there's no harm in it. Come on!"

"But I still don't know what to write," Flavius said miserably.

"I'll dictate to you," Julius offered.

Flavius sat down at the table, unrolled the parchment, smoothed it out, placed the candle beside it and picked up a charcoal pencil. Then he waited for Julius' dictation. Julius paced up and down pondering. Finally he stopped behind Flavius and began: "Dear Emperor." But that was as far as he got. Mucius and Publius instantly pounced on him.

"That's not the proper salutation for the Emperor," Mucius said.

"Then what is?" Julius asked, offended.

"I know," Antonius burst out. "Divine, merciful, glorious, revered, all-knowing Emperor."

"That's too much," Mucius said.

They quarreled about how the Emperor ought to be addressed; then they debated about every sentence as it was dictated to Flavius; and finally they argued about the signature. It took almost an hour before the letter was completed. But at last they were satisfied with it, and Flavius had to read it aloud several times.

"Most revered, divine Emperor," Flavius read, "we are petitioning you for mercy for Rufus, son of Praetonius. He is in prison accused of having written 'Caius is a dumbbell' on the wall of the temple of Minerva, which is dedicated to you. Rufus is innocent, for he was locked up in the Baths of Diana all night. He jumped into the pool through the opening in the roof. That must have been between the first and the second hours of the night. If he had jumped in when there was no water there, he would have been dead in the morning and could not have run away. The superintendent leaves at night and comes back in the morning. Meanwhile he drains the water and locks the door. Rufus was in there and could not get out. He ran past the superintendent in the morning and the superintendent thinks it was Mucius, but Mucius knows it was Rufus; for the superintendent found Mucius' lantern in the pool, but Rufus had the lantern with him, not Mucius. The two policemen said that 'Caius is a dumbbell' was not on the temple wall before the fifth hour of the night. They know that for certain, because that's the hour when they always get hungry and eat bread and figs and drink wine. The police always tell the truth. But 'Caius is a dumbbell' was on the temple wall before dawn. At that time Rufus was still locked in the Baths of Diana. That should prove that Rufus doesn't go around desecrating temples.

"Therefore we throw ourselves at your feet and ask for mercy for our friend Rufus.—The pupils of the Xanthos School."

Flavius stopped, out of breath.

"Couldn't be clearer," Mucius said, rubbing his hands with delight.

"Now we must hurry and deliver the letter to the palace," Julius said.

"Hold on. Haste makes waste," Publius warned. "Something else occurs to me. What about Scribonus?"

"What do you mean?" Mucius asked uneasily.

"Scribonus is the most famous handwriting expert in Rome," Publius said. "If Scribonus maintains that the writing is genuine, it is genuine."

"Hm," Julius murmured, and he began squinting at Mucius out of the corners of his eyes. Antonius and Flavius were also assailed by doubts once more. One or the other was telling the truth: Scribonus or

Mucius. But Scribonus was a famous scholar and Mucius was just a classmate.

Mucius sat down on a box again, propped his head on his clenched fists and stared into space.

"Maybe you only dreamed it all," Antonius said. "I have funny dreams sometimes, too. Last night I dreamed I was a pirate and fell into the water and I would have drowned if a dolphin hadn't . . ."

Furious, Mucius leaped to his feet and stuck Rufus' wet cloak under Antonius' nose. "There! Did I dream that?" he shouted. "And what about the lantern I found in the Baths of Diana?"

"The cloak smells bad," Antonius gasped, half smothered.

"Then don't talk such nonsense," Mucius said. "Rufus is innocent. That isn't a dream, that is the truth."

"But then who did the writing on the temple?" Julius asked. "The Emperor will want to know that, too."

"I can't know who wrote on the temple," Mucius cried, beside himself. "But somebody must have copied Rufus' handwriting."

"But who?" Julius repeated stubbornly.

"Maybe it was a ghost," Antonius said.

At that moment there was a crashing noise in

the dark corner of the cave, and a sullen voice said: "It was me."

The boys whirled around in fright. From back of the piles of junk, Caius emerged. He clambered over an upturned barrel. "I was the one who wrote 'Caius is a dumbbell' on the temple wall," he said, scowling at the boys.

15

Xantippus Finds the Point

"You?" the boys exclaimed.

"Yes," said Caius. "I copied his handwriting."

The boys clustered around him in excitement.

"What made you do it?" Mucius demanded.

"I wanted to get even."

"Then you were the one who broke into Xantippus' house?" Flavius cried.

Caius nodded.

"What did you hit him on the head with?" Antonius wanted to know.

"With my fist," Caius said.

"Did you also denounce Rufus to the prefect?" Mucius asked with terrible sternness.

"No, that wasn't me," Caius said. "I only wanted him to get a licking. I never thought he would be sent to prison."

At this point Publius pushed forward and asked

suspiciously: "How were you able to fake Rufus' handwriting so well?"

Caius hesitated for just a moment, then growled unwillingly: "I filled the grooves in the wax with red paint and pressed the tablet against the temple wall."

Publius was taken aback. "That's pretty slick," he admitted. The others were equally astonished; they never would have thought of so simple a trick. Only Julius sat pondering, a frown on his face.

"Caius isn't as dumb as we always thought," Publius said. "He even fooled Scribonus."

"He's lying," Julius said suddenly in a loud and decisive voice.

"I am not," Caius said uncertainly.

"You are so lying!" Julius retorted. "You didn't copy Rufus' handwriting at all. If you had filled the grooves in the wax with red paint and pressed the wax tablet against the wall like you say, the writing would have come out turned around. I can prove it to you. Look at this!" he told the others, and went to the table. Taking the piece of charcoal with which Flavius had written the letter to the Emperor, he crumpled it, spat vigorously into the bits several times, and with his fingers kneaded the mass into a black pulp. Then he rushed to the corner and came back with a smooth piece of board. Sticking his forefinger into the charcoal paste, he wrote the word CAIUS on the board. Then he pressed the board firmly upon the white marble tabletop, lifted it and triumphantly showed them the result. On the marble top they could see distinctly, though rather smearily, the word ꙄUIAꙄ.

Mucius turned around and studied Caius with great seriousness. "Will you explain, please, why you said you did it, when you didn't?" he asked sternly.

Caius stood with compressed lips. But abruptly he turned red and said, "Take me to the prefect and tell him I did it. Then Rufus will be released."

"Oho, so that's the way the wind blows!" Publius cried scornfully.

"I suppose you're sorry now that you tattled to your father about Rufus?" Mucius said.

Caius nodded. "It's my fault he's in prison," he muttered guiltily.

"Well, it's decent of you to admit it," Julius observed with more friendliness.

"Let's be nice to him again," Flavius said. "He's sorry about it all."

"I'm not sorry about anything," Caius mumbled crossly. "I want to be taken back in the gang again. That's all."

"We haven't any time to be playing," Mucius said. "We have to find out who copied Rufus' handwriting; otherwise Rufus is done for."

"I know," Caius murmured with downcast eyes. "I heard the whole thing. The reason I hid was because I wanted to know what you fellows were saying about me. How do you know that somebody faked the handwriting?"

"That's just what we can't prove," Mucius said. "Nobody will believe us. People will believe Scribonus."

"Maybe there's some trick to it," Caius said, scratching himself behind the ear. He looked anything but bright as he did so.

"Or magic," Antonius suggested.

At the word "trick" Julius had looked up and fixed his eyes on Caius with a cunning expression. "How did you happen to think up that story of the paint and the grooves of the wax?" he asked. "Did you hit on that all by yourself?"

"I once watched the way our cook baked cookies," Caius replied. "The cookies were all shaped like letters. That was a long time ago, but it made a big impression on me. He had wooden molds which were shaped like letters. He placed the molds on a bronze platter; then he poured the dough into the grooves of the letters and put the platter in the oven. When he took the platter out later and lifted the molds, there were the baked letters right on the platter. He gave them to me so I could learn to read, but I ate them."

"Heavenly gods, help me!" Julius murmured, overwhelmed. "I bet I have it."

"Have what?"

"Of course, that's the way it was done. No other way possible," Julius moaned.

"He's gone out of his mind," Flavius said.

"An evil spirit has got into him," Antonius said.

"Let him talk!" Mucius shouted at them.

"I know how Rufus' writing was copied," Julius said. "Someone pierced through the letters on his wax tablet, then pressed the tablet against the wall and ran a brush dipped in red paint over the grooves. That way 'Caius is a dumbbell' would appear on the wall just the way Rufus wrote it."

It took a while for the others to grasp what he meant, but then they all cheered him loudly. Julius had solved the mystery. Flavius and Antonius danced with joy. Mucius pounded Julius on the back. "You're a genius!" he praised him.

Caius alone had not understood a word of the explanation, but no one had expected him to. Even Publius had nothing to criticize this time. "I had a hunch it was something of the sort," he said with a grin.

"Let's have that letter," Mucius said. "We must add this explanation. Rufus will certainly be freed today."

Flavius had to sit down at the table again and Julius and Mucius began dictating the postscript about the forging of the script. But before Flavius could finish the last sentence, they heard a well-known voice at the entrance saying, "So I've finally caught up with you scoundrels!" And in hobbled Xantippus, leaning on a stick.

The boys gaped. Xantippus himself in person! What could have made him seek them out in their cave. Certainly nothing pleasant. And sure enough, Xantippus was in anything but a sweet temper. "If Rompus hadn't told me you might be in your cave I would never have found you," he scolded. "Lovely tales I've been hearing!" Groaning, he limped toward them, paused and looked around for a seat. Mucius hastily took a box and offered it to their teacher.

Xantippus cautiously settled down on the box and glanced around with a frown of disapproval, for the cave was not exactly a model of neatness. Then he went on: "Rufus' mother and Rompus came to see me. They had the idea you might be at school,

but of course you weren't to be found. Livia told me
about this sorry mess with Rufus—a terrible thing,
terrible. There isn't much I can do, since I am not
a Roman citizen, but I assured her of my support.
My leg still hurts like the devil, but I went looking

for you. I had to rent a sedan chair with two bearers. They're waiting for me outside, and every minute is costing me money. So hurry up. What did Lukos say?"

The boys remained shamefacedly silent. Finally Julius murmured, "For some reason, Lukos wouldn't use his second sight for us."

"But we found out for ourselves that Rufus is innocent," Mucius declared proudly.

"So you have, have you?" Xantippus said. "You might have taken the trouble to let Livia know— leaving that poor woman in suspense all this time— is that nice?"

"We wrote a letter to the Emperor first," Julius said.

Xantippus raised his bushy eyebrows. "You wrote a letter to the Emperor!"

"We wanted to show that Rufus is completely innocent and asked for a pardon for him," Mucius said.

"Where is this fine letter of yours?"

"Here." Mucius handed their teacher the book on which Flavius had written the letter. Xantippus moved closer to the light, unrolled the parchment and began to read: "How long, O Catiline, will you continue to abuse our patience? How long will you continue to mock us with your madness? Will your unbridled impudence never cease?" He broke off, stared mystified at his pupils and asked, "What is the meaning of this? Why do you drag in Cicero's oration?"

"That happens to be a copy of Cicero," Mucius said. "Our letter's on the back."

"You might have told me that in the first place," Xantippus growled irritably. He turned the roll over and silently read the letter. Then he looked up and asked darkly, "Who wrote this?"

"I did," Flavius admitted.

"A frightful piece of work," Xantippus snarled. "Swarming with mistakes. Your spelling is disgraceful. I'll see about this when school begins again!"

He tossed the parchment roll on the table. "Furthermore, your logic is full of holes and your proofs are worthless," he continued. "I am not surprised that you are all so bad in mathematics. Sit down."

The boys obediently took seats on the boxes. No place was left for Flavius and he had to sit on the floor.

"Does any one of you have the faintest recollection of Pythagoras?" Xantippus asked.

The boys nodded eagerly, although they no longer remembered what Pythagoras was all about.

"In a right-angle triangle the square of the hypotenuse equals the sum of the squares of the two sides. What do we call such a statement?" Xantippus asked.

"A riddle," Caius mumbled.

Xantippus gave him a withering look, then turned contemptuously away and called: "Julius!"

"A proof," Julius replied.

"Wrong," Xantippus said. "It is a hypothesis. A hypothesis is a statement which must be proved before it is accepted as true. The so-called proofs in your letter are nothing more than hypotheses. Did anyone see Rufus in the Baths of Diana?"

"No," Mucius admitted.

"Then you have no witnesses, and without witnesses you can prove nothing. Now about the forging of the script. It is possible that Rufus' writing tablet was used as a pattern, but who is to say that Rufus himself did not do it?"

Julius raised his hand.

"Yes?" Xantippus said.

"Why should Rufus go to all the trouble of piercing through the wax when all he had to do was write on the wall?"

"Have you ever tried writing in the dark?" Xantippus asked.

Julius had not thought of that.

"You see!" Xantippus said complacently. "You don't even write well by light."

The other boys laughed. Julius looked insulted.

"Quiet!" Xantippus commanded. "I am not here to amuse you."

"Then do you think Rufus is guilty?" Mucius asked timidly.

Xantippus suddenly flew into a rage. The veins stood out on his temples. "Did I say that?" he barked.

"No-o," Mucius stammered.

"Then don't ask such silly questions." Xantippus stared down at the tabletop, pondering, and the boys did not dare to stir. They were waiting for more hard words and sarcastic questions. Livia should have known better than to get Xantippus into this. He couldn't believe that anything they did was any good. All he could do was interfere.

When Xantippus looked up again, however, he seemed to be in a somewhat milder mood. "I know Rufus and he isn't the kind of boy who goes around defacing temples," he said. "We'll save him yet."

The boys' spirits rose. Xantippus was capable of human emotion after all. Delighted, Mucius cried out, "We've been racking our brains trying to think who really did it."

Xantippus said pedantically, "You have no doubt

overlooked the very point that may give us a lead. Mucius, tell me once more, and very carefully, all that you have so far learned about the whole affair in regard to Rufus. I want every little point. Even something that seems unimportant may give us a clue."

Mucius stood up as if he were in class, took a deep breath, and began somewhat clumsily to tell the story. But as he went on he gained assurance—he gave a blow-by-blow description of everything that had happened since the fateful quarrel between Rufus and Caius—what he had done and what the other boys had done—what they had discovered—what conclusions they had drawn. Now for the first time he saw some use in all the drill that Xantippus had given them in the art of public speaking.

When he had finished, Xantippus nodded approval. "Take your seat!" he said.

Mucius sat down. Xantippus reflected for a while. Then he pounded his stick twice against the rocky floor of the cave and said, "We have our point to stand on."

The boys stared at him in suspense.

"Our point is the newspaper report," Xantippus went on. "What occurred to you when you read the report about the defacing of the temple?"

"Nothing," Julius confessed.

"We were angry," Flavius said.

"On the contrary, you should have been pleased," Xantippus declared. "The newspaper report proves to us that Rufus is not guilty, that, in fact, he is completely innocent."

"Why?" the boys chorused.

"Because the newspaper report was written before the defacing of the temple was committed," Xantippus said. "Do you understand?"

The boys did not.

"Then I shall have to explain this simple matter to you." Xantippus sighed. "The Censor's office, which publishes the newspaper, does not open until the third hour of the day. The first task of the officials is to post the morning newspaper in the Forum. But the reports for the newspaper are written the night before. You see, they are written in script, and that requires much time and trouble. If the officials only began in the morning, it would be very late before the first edition of the newspaper appeared. Therefore one copyist and one official to receive reports always remain in the office at night until the fourth or at the latest the fifth hour, in order to gather material and write the stories. I myself once worked in the Censor's office for several years, so I know exactly what the procedure is. Sometimes couriers with especially important news items arrive late at night. These items are published the next day. Now the item about the defacing of the temple appeared in the first morning edition; that means that it must have been delivered at the Censor's office by the fourth hour of the night at the latest. I hope all this is penetrating your thick skulls so that I won't have to repeat it ten times."

The boys nodded assent. They were gradually beginning to realize how the newspaper report fitted into the mystery, although they still did not see how it would help them track down the real culprit.

"According to the testimony of the two policemen," Xantippus continued, "there was nothing on the temple wall before the fifth hour of the night. Accordingly, the newspaper report was written before the defacing of the temple. And that should give us something to think about."

"Couldn't this have been an exception and the item added to the bulletin in the morning?" Julius asked.

"Such exceptions do occur when there is news of really unusual importance—which this was not," Xantippus stated. "But we have even clearer evidence that no such exception was made for this particular item. Mucius said that the report was about in the middle of the newspaper, among many other reports. Is that right?"

"Yes," the boys chorused.

"That proves that it could not have been added in the morning, or it would have been placed on an extra board. Besides which, the item was unusually long. Most news items are published in very brief form, especially the extras. The officials therefore must have taken time to write it out in full. The length of the report, moreover, suggests that it was sent by a very important personage, so that the officials did not dare to shorten it."

Xantippus stood up and began hobbling back and forth, leaning on his stick. "We therefore have to consider the following points," he continued. "How did this important personage know that 'Caius is a dumbbell' was going to be written on the temple wall? What was his interest in seeing that the incident was reported in the newspaper? Why was suspicion so obviously pointed toward the pupils of the Xanthos School? And finally: Who is this personage? This last question is the first matter we have to discover. That ought not to be too difficult. For example, if we know which courier delivered the report at the Censor's office, we can find out who sent him. I am unfortunately out of commission; my leg hurts and I must go back home and lie down again. You boys will have to find out who the courier was. Go to the Censor's office and ask to speak to the official who receives the night reports. Ask him which courier brought the item about the defacing of the temple. Then come to me at once and we will see what our next step is. But kindly hurry up this time and don't waste your time on idle talk and silly letter-writing. Good luck!" He hobbled off toward the exit.

"What will we do if the report was delivered by an unknown courier?" Julius called after him.

Xantippus turned around. "No official would accept a report from an unknown courier. The couriers must carry credentials with them. Any official who publishes a false story can be punished by death. And now don't ask so many questions! Get to work." Xantippus disappeared through the curtain, and the boys hurried after him.

Outside the bearers, two powerful Arabs, were waiting with their sedan chair. Xantippus climbed in and ordered them to carry him back to Broad Street. The bearers energetically shouldered the chair and started off at a trot along the narrow path. Xantippus thrust his head out once more and called to the boys: "You had better clean up your cave. It's a regular pigsty!" Then he disappeared around a turning.

"We didn't invite him," Publius remarked.

"Did you understand everything he said?" Caius asked.

"I shudder to think of what we'll be in for when school starts again," Flavius said, sighing.

"If you ask me, Xantippus has been pretty decent," Julius commented. "He's really trying to be of help."

"I guess he's sorry he treated Rufus so badly," Flavius said.

"He's really smart," Julius said appreciatively. "We never would have thought about that newspaper business."

"The important personage must be a whopping big crook," Antonius said.

"Are we really going to the Censor's office?" Flavius asked, worriedly.

"Of course," Mucius said. "And right away. Let's go! Follow me!" He started off, taking great leaps down the steep slope.

16

Cheap Soap, Burned Oil, and Onions

The boys had to go twice around the State Archives Building on the Forum before they found, on a quiet side lane, the entrance to the Censor's office. At the door stood an armed guard, a tough-looking young man.

"What are you kids after?" he asked harshly.

Mucius repeated the formula they had decided on. "We must speak to the Censor's officials," he said as innocently as possible.

"What's your business with them?" the guard asked, leaning indifferently against the wall. He took off his helmet and wiped his brow, for the day had grown rather warm.

"We are bringing an important message," Mucius lied with a straight face.

"A sensational story," Antonius added, nodding vigorously.

"Do you have credentials?" the guard asked, plunking his helmet on his head.

"We don't need any," Mucius said. "The story is about us."

"Then go to the devil," the guard said without interest.

The boys retreated to a shady corner under the colonnades of the State Archives Building, where they could keep an eye on the guard. Their plan had fallen flat. By all their calculations, the guard should have admitted them when they claimed to have important news. Now they would have to think up something else.

Caius, whom they had taken along on a probation basis, suggested pushing the guard aside and running into the building. "If you don't care to try it, I'll do it by myself," he said, throwing fierce looks at the brawny fellow lounging in the doorway.

"You think you're a Hercules," Publius scoffed.

"No violence," Mucius said. "That would spoil everything. We must use our heads."

Julius nodded. "Let's tell him the truth," he proposed, rubbing his nose thoughtfully.

"You do that!" Mucius decided.

They approached the entrance again. The guard had sat down on the base of a column and was lovingly polishing his sword, which already gleamed like a metal mirror in the sunlight. He looked up in surprise as the boys trooped up to him once more. "So you're here again?" he said.

"We have a great favor to beg of you," Julius began flatteringly.

"Yes?" the guard asked skeptically. "Listen, kids, I'm just on guard here. I can't do anything for you."

"We would not ask you to," Julius said, standing on his dignity. "All we wanted to do was check something with the official who takes the late news at night."

"Do you mean Megabates?" the guard said.

"Yes, he's the one we mean," Publius grinned.

"A Greek, isn't he?" Mucius asked quickly. He recognized Megabates as a Greek name.

"Can we see him?" Julius asked.

"Megabates isn't around yet," the guard replied. "He's on night duty, so he gets his sleep in the morning."

"He doesn't live far from here, does he?" Julius asked at hazard.

"If you know him so well, you must know his address, too," the guard said, slyly.

"Of course we know his address," Antonius burst out. "It's just slipped our minds. Sometimes we almost forget where our school is."

The guard laughed. He liked the boys. It wasn't too long ago since he himself had played hookey from school on a spring day. "Megabates lives in a house on Patrician Street, right on the corner of Subura," he said. "But now clear out of here!" he roared good-naturedly, and he jokingly raised his sword.

"Thank you very much," the boys called as they ran off, in high spirits. They turned the corner and were once more in the Forum. The big square was swarming with people who had been lured out by the warmth of this first real spring day. The sun was shining, the sky was a brilliant blue, and a gentle breeze which smelled of spring blew from the south. Everybody looked happy, and the dazzling white togas and tunics the people wore showed that they had fetched out their finest clothes to celebrate so fine a day. But the boys weren't out for a leisurely promenade. They plowed their way through the crowd, using their elbows to good purpose. As they pushed on, Mucius glanced at the gloomy city jail at the foot of the Capitol. "There's where Rufus is," he said, stopping in his tracks.

The others stared at the prison.

"It must be awful in there," Flavius murmured.

"The prisoners are kept deep underground," Antonius said.

"Maybe we could dig a tunnel and free Rufus," Caius proposed.

Publius laughed at him. "Where would you start to dig?" he asked. "Right here in the Forum, in front of the whole world?"

Caius took offense. "All you can ever do is make silly jokes," he snorted, starting toward him.

"It's just that you're too dumb to understand them," Publius retorted, clenching his fists.

"Shut up!" Mucius warned, stepping between them. "People are staring at us. If you want to fight, do it when you're alone."

The boys moved on. They made their way to the Senate building, took a less crowded side street and soon reached the gorge known as the Subura. As they approached the corner of Patrician Street, they saw the building the guard must have referred to.

It was a shabby, five-story tenement. The lower story consisted entirely of wretched little stores, mere niches in the building, with goods spread out on the sidewalk. On the corner was a barber's booth. The barber was standing in the street cutting a customer's hair with an enormous pair of shears. The man sat submissively on a stool, and a group of street boys stood around, following the proceedings with interest. Next door there was a butcher shop. The meat hung on big hooks set into the wall. Then came a booth with a goat's head carved in stone above the entrance, indicating that this was where milk was sold. After that came a laundry, a vegetable shop, and a dirty tavern.

The boys wondered how to get into the building, since they saw no entrance. Finally Mucius asked the barber where the door was.

"Around the back," the barber said, jerking his shears over his shoulder toward Patrician Street.

At the corner of the building the boys struck a narrow, well-trodden path, evidently much used by the rightful inhabitants of the place. This path led into the backyard, and from there the tenement did not look quite so ugly as from the front. Along all the stories ran roofed galleries from which at intervals tiny open balconies projected. Assorted potted plants sent forth vines and greenery which jutted and trailed over the railings of the balconies. Wooden steps led from the yard up to the galleries. The yard itself was paved with large flagstones, and there was a fountain in the center of it. Off to one side three small girls were jumping rope. They stopped playing when the well-dressed boys came in, and gaped in wonder.

The boys strolled toward the building and took the staircase whose steps were worn smooth by much traffic.

"I'll bet nothing but criminals live here," Antonius said.

"You're letting your imagination run away again," Julius said. "This is the kind of place where craftsmen, shopkeepers, and freed slaves live. The majority of them are Greeks and Arabs; they are not criminals."

This was the first time the boys had ever entered a tenement house, and they felt like explorers. On the lowest gallery they stopped in confusion. A number of doorways covered only by curtains led to the interior of the building. From behind these curtains they could hear all sorts of noises—dishes rattling, children whining, shrill women's and hoarse men's voices quarreling. Dogs were barking, and somewhere a young man was crooning a sentimental song. There was a smell of cheap soap, burned oil, and onions.

"I feel sick to my stomach," Flavius murmured.

"No backing down now," Mucius said.

"We'll never find Megabates in this hive," Flavius said.

"We'll have to ask," Mucius said, and boldly pulled aside the nearest curtain. They found themselves themselves looking into a tiny kitchen. A sturdy woman was standing over a steaming trough, scrubbing clothes on a wooden board. She looked up, her face flushed with heat and annoyance, and shouted, "Get out of here, you rascals."

The boys hastily withdrew.

A little old man clad in rags came along the gallery toward them, walking unsteadily. The boys approached him. "Where does Megabates live?" they asked.

The old man chuckled and started to babble at great length—the boys did not understand so much as a syllable of his speech. He smelled strongly of wine, which made them uneasy. But he seemed eager to be of help, for he went on chattering and pointing upward with a dirty finger.

"I guess Megabates lives further up," Mucius said to his friends.

"But where?" Publius asked. "On the roof?"

"Wait, I have an idea!" Julius said, turning to Publius. "Do any of you happen to have a charcoal pencil with you?"

"I do," said Publius, producing one from the pocket of his tunic.

Julius took possession of the pencil and went over to the wall, calling "Hey, you!" to the old man. The man looked at him with a vacant smile. Julius waved the pencil in the air to hold the old fellow's attention; then he drew on the wall a staircase, and after it put a large question mark.

The old man realized what Julius wanted, took the pencil from him and made five long dashes beside the question mark. Under these he placed three small dashes. Then he pocketed the pencil and reeled off down the stairs. The boys saw him staggering across the yard, heading for the tavern.

"My pencil!" Publius protested.

"Let him keep the pencil," Mucius said. "The old boy has done us a service."

"How come?" Caius wanted to know. "What are those marks supposed to mean?"

The others laughed at his slowness.

"Megabates lives on the fifth floor, you idiot," Julius explained.

"But what are the three small dashes for?" Flavius asked.

"Maybe the third door," Mucius said hopefully.

He had guessed right, for now they noticed that all the doorways were numbered. They climbed the wooden steps to the fifth gallery, where they stopped in front of the door marked III. Mucius pounded his fist against the curtain, but this action produced no sound at all, merely a dense cloud of dust. Then he called out, "Does Megabates live here?" Whereupon a cross voice replied, "Come in!"

"I don't think we need take off our sandals here," Mucius whispered to the others as he entered.

Apparently the newspaperman's job was not very highly paid. Megabates' apartment consisted of a single poorly furnished, windowless room. In one corner was a small open fireplace in which a fire was burning; in the other corner a straw pallet lay on the floor—probably the bed. Along the walls were nails from which hung clothing and blankets.

Megabates was seated at the table with a steaming bowl of peas and sausage which he was eating slowly. Beside the bowl lay a large piece of bread and a broad-bladed, daggerlike knife. The Censor's official was a rather pinched-looking elderly man whose pointed gray beard reminded the boys of Xantippus. He went right on with his meal. Finally he growled, with full mouth, "Who are you?"

"Are you Megabates?" Mucius asked.

"What do you want?"

"We have something very important to discuss with you," Mucius said.

"I am Megabates, but I cannot discuss anything now," Megabates growled, completely absorbed in his peas and sausage.

"Forgive us for disturbing you, but we are in a great hurry," Mucius apologized.

"I'm in a hurry, too," Megabates said. "I must get to my office. Come back tomorrow." This seemed to settle the affair as far as he was concerned, for with his fingers he lifted another chunk of sausage to his mouth.

Mucius did not give up. "We only wanted to know whether you received the news reports night before last at the Censor's office," he said.

"I did," Megabates said indistinctly, his mouth full. "What concern is it of yours?"

"We should like to know who the courier was who brought the item about the desecration of the temple," Mucius said.

"That's confidential information," Megabates said curtly. He sharpened the knife on the edge of the bowl and cut himself a thick slice of bread.

"Please tell us!" Mucius pleaded.

"Who are you anyway?" Megabates demanded.

"Mucius Marius Domitius."

Megabates looked up, startled. "Domitius? Are you by any chance related to his excellency, the honorable tribune Domitius?"

"He is my father," Mucius said as modestly as possible.

Megabates jumped up, choked down his mouthful of bread and bowed low. "Forgive me, young sir! Why didn't you say so at once? Has your father sent you?"

Mucius nodded. A lie at a time like this didn't really count. After all, his friend's life was at stake.

"My father is Senator Vinicius," Caius blurted out.

Megabates, bowed to him also. "Of course, of course," he stammered, confused. "Any information which is in my power to give," he agreed eagerly. "Let me think. Night before last . . . the report on the desecration of the temple . . . Ah yes, I remember now. The courier came rather late, around the fourth hour of the night . . ."

The boys threw significant glances at one another. Xantippus had guessed correctly.

"He brought a sealed letter," Megabates continued, "with the words 'very urgent' on the outside. I opened the letter and found the report on the desecration of the temple. It was written in shorthand, but it was long, extremely long, and was therefore a great nuisance to us. I personally would have liked to have told the courier to get out . . ."

"Why didn't you?" Antonius asked.

"Why, how could I do that?" Megabates exclaimed in alarm. "The courier was sent by his excellency Ex-consul Tellus!"

"Ex-consul Tellus?" the boys cried in amazement.

"Yes," Megabates said. "By Ex-consul Tellus in person."

17

A Certain Guest

Xantippus was as amazed as the boys when he heard the identity of the man who had sent the courier.

Many years ago Ex-consul Tellus had been a famous general who defeated the Persians and Armenians and half a dozen other oriental tribes. After a number of campaigns he had returned home a hero, and with the millions he had gained in booty, retired to private life. Since then his fame had somewhat faded, but he kept some sort of reputation alive by the expensive parties he gave in his huge palace in the gardens of Lucullus. Nevertheless, he was not popular; he was feared for his malicious tongue and for his tremendous influence in social life and politics. He was a close friend of all the highest dignitaries, and it was said that the Emperor himself had great faith in Tellus and told him all his plans.

Xantippus sat in his room, surrounded by books,

papers, compasses, rulers, and other geometrical instruments.

"Tellus?" he said, placing his injured leg on a hassock. "Tellus! This certainly is a surprise! Of course it beautifully confirms my theory about an important personage, but to tell the truth I hadn't counted on anyone quite that important. Well, if it's so, it's so. We must not be put off by this. Let us consider this turn of events with cool heads, my young friends."

The boys grinned, flattered. This was the first time Xantippus had ever offered to discuss a subject with the boys on a basis of equality.

"It seems unlikely that Tellus has any connection with the crime," Xantippus said. "What reason could an ex-consul have for engineering a crime to throw suspicion upon young Rufus?"

Antonius spoke up. "Maybe he was envious because Rufus' father just won such a great victory over the Gauls. Generals are always jealous of each other. Pompey wanted to kill Caesar, Caesar wanted to kill Pompey, and afterwards Brutus killed Caesar and Anthony killed Brutus, and my father knew a general who even killed himself because he was mad when another general won a battle . . ."

"That's enough," Xantippus interrupted him. "You can tell us about that during the history lesson.

It is quite true that jealousy and envy will drive people to the most illogical actions, but Tellus himself was so successful a general that he does not have to begrudge his colleague Praetonius a victory. Besides, at the time of the defacing of the temple nobody in Rome knew anything about the victory; otherwise the news of it would have appeared in the morning newspaper. So the culprit must have had other motives. And for that reason I scarcely believe it was Tellus. A little reasoning should make that clear. Tellus is a person who lives only for his pleasure. And it is no pleasure to steal through the dark streets of Rome at night, to knock out harmless teachers, rob them, then smear up sacred buildings. Tellus can afford amusements of another sort. Furthermore, Tellus is a friend and intimate of the Emperor. He would certainly think twice about risking this position of trust he now occupies, for he of all people would know the Emperor does not take kindly to such jokes. And finally, how could Tellus have known that Caius and Rufus quarreled and that Rufus' writing tablet was here in school? Shall I assume that one of you ran off to him and told him all about it?"

"No, no!" the boys protested.

Xantippus tugged at his pointed beard. "Well then, you see that it cannot have been Tellus."

"Hypothesis," Publius murmured in a low voice.

Fortunately Xantippus did not hear him. "We will now consider the situation in another light," he continued. "Tellus sent the courier; there is no doubt about that. Nobody would dare to misuse the name of the mighty ex-consul. But Tellus may well have acted as the unsuspecting agent for the real culprit. A person living the way he does has many hangers-on. It is well known that he is a great admirer of actors, dancers, acrobats, and other such characters. Now I happen to know that the night of the desecration of the temple Tellus gave one of his disgusting feasts. There is therefore the following possibility: One of his guests may have started the rumor of the desecration of the temple, and have persuaded Tellus to send the courier to the newspaper. He would know that Tellus, as a friend of the Emperor, would feel bound to make a fuss. The man lied, of course, for the temple had not yet been defaced. But then later he must have secretly slipped away from the banquet in order to commit the crime. Possibly he had had no chance to do it before. But he also wanted to cast suspicion on Rufus right from the start and therefore he persuaded Tellus to send the report to the newspaper before the Censor's office closed. Our next task is therefore: Who was this guest?"

Publius spoke up. "Tellus' parties are always so large that we might just as well look for the criminal in the Forum."

"Sarcasm gets us nowhere," Xantippus reproved him. "You are only trying to make up by impudence for a lack of intelligence. I know that Tellus' parties are very large, but the guest we are looking for will have certain distinguishing marks. For one thing, the route between his home and the palace of Tellus must have run by the temple of Minerva; otherwise he could not claim to have discovered the alleged desecration of the temple. When a man tells a lie like that, he must take care to make it plausible."

"But it was dark then. How could he have seen anything?" Caius asked.

"A rich man out at night is accompanied by many slaves with torches and lanterns," Xantippus said. "And Tellus' guests are all rich. Naturally there was nothing written on the temple at the time he passed, since he did it himself later on. The slaves also saw nothing, but then they probably knew nothing about his lie to Ex-consul Tellus." Xantippus got up and hobbled over to a map of Rome which hung on the wall. "Now look," he said. "To grasp the significance of this you must follow me closely. Tellus' palace is over here in the Gardens of Lucullus. Tellus' guests are high dignitaries, and almost all of them live near the Imperial Palace on the Palatine Hill. Their route, as you can see, leads directly across the Forum, past the Capitol and along Broad Street to the Gardens of Lucullus. Nobody would take the foolish roundabout route uphill and down across the Esquiline Hill, especially not at night. Guests who live on the Viminalis or Quirinalis are ruled out at the start, since the temple of Minerva is in the opposite direction. Therefore the question narrows down to those who live on the Esquiline Hill itself. But even at that, the temple of Minerva is so out of the way that only two or three of them could possibly pass it. We can therefore confine our attention to a very small number of persons." Xantippus limped back to his easy chair and sat down.

The boys were much impressed by this exposition, but they did not know how to go on from there.

"What if the guest himself did not do it, but ordered one of his slaves to," Julius suggested.

Xantippus shook his head. "That is practically out of the question," he said. "You all know the proverb: 'The most dangerous part of a slave is his tongue.' No rich man would entrust a slave with an important secret unless he could not help himself. He would be too afraid of the slave's talking, or using blackmail. A rich man has to commit his own crimes if he wants to sleep peacefully."

This, too, struck the boys as sound reasoning. But how were they ever going to pin the blame on the mysterious guest, for all that Xantippus had so cleverly narrowed a circle around him. There still were a great many people living in the vicinity of the temple of Minerva. The boys could not very well go from door to door asking, "Excuse us, please, but are you the man who wrote 'Caius is a dumbbell' on the temple wall?"

"Why don't we just go to Tellus and ask him?" Mucius proposed.

But Xantippus was opposed to that. "That wouldn't help us at all and might even lead to trouble," he said. "Tellus is friends with everybody who counts. He would not want to offend anyone, and will therefore answer no questions. Tellus is a politician, and in politics one hand washes the other."

"We won't ever find the man then," Julius said, losing heart. "All we can do is ask the help of the gods. We ought to bring them a sacrifice."

"Well now, there's no use running to unnecessary expense," Xantippus countered. "The gods help those who help themselves. For the present we can try another plan. And I happen to know another fact about Tellus which will be useful to us. Although Tellus gives the impression of caring for nothing but pleasure, he is really always looking out for his personal future. A politician never knows whether he may not fall into disgrace some day, and at such times it is well to have old friends to depend on. But when things are going badly for a man, old friends have a way of forgetting their friendship. Tellus is cunning. He has a sort of guest book, and asks all his guests to sign their names in it; naturally each of them feels honored when the rich and famous ex-consul makes such a request. But Tellus' guest book is not just an ordinary scroll which might be lost or destroyed; it is a white marble wall in the great hall of his palace. Tellus has had a special red paint made which is not washable, and the guests paint their names on the wall with a brush. Over each list of names is placed the date of the feast at which the guests were present. That is very handy for us, since the name of the guest we are interested in will be under the twentieth of March."

"But how can we get a look at this guest list?" Mucius asked.

"I have a plan in mind," Xantippus replied. "But it hinges on someone's being able to commit to memory all the names. There may have been fifteen, twenty or even more guests at this affair. Which of you has a good memory?"

"Me!" Antonius burst out. "I have a terrific memory. I even remember when I lay in my cradle. It was awful. I couldn't talk yet; all I could say was 'Father' and 'Mother.' That made me so mad that I cried all the time."

"That is not any special feat of memory," Xantippus said dryly. "I, too, remember lying in my cradle."

The boys broke into peals of laughter. There was something irresistibly funny about the idea of Xantippus' ever having been a baby.

"Quiet!" Xantippus snapped. "If you want to laugh, do it at home or in the streets. I will not have laughter in my presence."

Julius spoke up. "Antonius really does have a good memory. He only has to read something once and he knows it by heart."

"If that is so, why does he never know his lists of Greek words?" Xantippus commented.

"That's because he never looks at them," Caius murmured.

"Are you all of the opinion that Antonius has the best memory among you?" Xantippus asked.

"Yes!" the boys agreed—Antonius joining the chorus.

1 7 9

"All right then," Xantippus said, not very enthusiastically. "Then we have no choice; we must send him to Tellus."

"Me?" Antonius cried, overwhelmed.

"You are to take him a letter from me," Xantippus said. "A few years ago I did some historical research for Tellus, so that he knows me. I will write and ask him to put in a good word for Rufus with the Emperor. He will toss my petition into his wastebasket unread, but that does not matter. You take the letter to the palace and say you are to wait for an answer. Here are ten sesterces. Give them to the doorkeeper so that he will let you in. He will lead you into the great hall, where the marble wall with the list of names is, and while the letter is being taken to Tellus and you are waiting for the reply you will have time enough to look for the names under the twentieth of March and to learn them by heart. But then hurry straight back here and don't linger on the way. When we have the names we will know where the people live; it will then be easy to find the man we want."

Xantippus hastily wrote a few lines on a parchment, rolled it up, and gave it to Antonius. "All right, be off with you. You should be back within an hour at the latest."

"I'll be back a lot sooner than that," Antonius said, and scooted out the door.

"Why can't we all go?" Mucius asked in disappointment.

"More than one would make for awkwardness," Xantippus said. "Besides, you would only distract Antonius. He must be free to concentrate completely on the names."

"So now we have to sit around here for an hour doing nothing," Caius said grumpily.

"I should think not," Xantippus snapped. "As long as you are here you may just as well learn something. Where, by the way, is the homework I assigned you?"

"Homework?" Caius asked, pretending innocence.

"You were supposed to write out the Greek words in fair hand ten times."

"Oh, that . . ." Caius mumbled. "I was sick."

"So you were sick, were you?" Xantippus mimicked him. "Too bad. You are looking very well today. Here is a tablet and a stylus—go into the schoolroom and get to work. And you others, you can each take a volume of Sallust from my shelf over there and study a little Roman history."

The boys picked out the books, went into the

classroom, and sat down on the benches. Caius stared unhappily down at his writing tablet. He no longer had the slightest idea what Greek words he was supposed to write. The others were not in a very industrious mood either. They'd never liked Sallust anyway, and their minds were on Antonius. What a shame, each boy was thinking, that it was Antonius who had the best memory, and not himself.

18

A Banquet

Strangely, Antonius remained away much more than an hour. His friends were fuming mad, because all the time he was away they had to sit boring themselves with Sallust. They looked out on the street more than they did at their books, and now and then one of them would dash outside to see whether Antonius was in sight yet.

When two hours had passed, Xantippus also grew uneasy and called the boys in. "I had my doubts from the start about entrusting Antonius with so important a mission," he said. "Probably he is lazing around the Forum looking at shops. If he doesn't come soon, you will have to go out to look for him."

But no sooner had he spoken than the curtain was pulled aside and Antonius appeared in the doorway. He presented an amazing appearance. Perched askew on his head was a crushed wreath of flowers which had slipped down over his forehead. His sandals were missing, and over his shoulders hung a man's cloak that was far too big for him. "Hello, my friends," he greeted them. "If you only knew what I've been through! Hahaha!" He started singing, spread out his arms, and whirled in a circle.

"You good-for-nothing rascal, what have you been up to?" Xantippus thundered.

Antonius pulled the cloak from his shoulders and held it out to Xantippus. "The cloak . . . the chain . . ." he stammered. "Here's the chain you pulled off the burglar's neck."

From the collar of the cloak dangled the golden chain the boys had found under the wardrobe.

"So it is," Xantippus murmured in amazement. "This is it. You can even see the place where the hook was straightened out." He fixed Antonius with a questioning look. "To whom does this cloak belong?"

"Tellus," Antonius said.

Xantippus frowned. "What?" he cried out. "How did you come by Tellus' cloak?"

"It's the strangest story you ever heard!" Antonius began to laugh.

"Did you go to see Tellus at all?" Mucius asked.

"Of course," Antonius replied. "It was marvel-

ous. I had a wonderful time. At the end they even wanted to kill me!"

"Tell us, tell us! What happened?" all the boys cried at once.

"Where are the names?" Julius asked.

"I don't have them. They weren't listed."

Xantippus was still staring at the cloak and chain, shaking his head. "How do you know this is Tellus' cloak?" he asked.

"I stole it from his bedroom," Antonius replied.

"How in the world did you get into Tellus' bedroom?"

"Well, it was this way," Antonius began. "Tellus

had visitors. There were eight gentlemen with him. They were sprawling around the table on couches and eating. The doorman didn't want to let me in, so I gave him the letter and the ten sesterces, and then he told me to wait. He left me outside in front of the door, and I was mad because he didn't take me into the great hall. But a few minutes later Tellus himself came waddling toward me, the letter in his hand. He's small and fat and bald, and there's a big scar on his head. He was wearing a golden laurel wreath and looked like Bacchus. Right away he was nice to me as could be; he said he was so happy to meet me, and asked me in. I said I was happy, too, and started looking for the marble wall. But Tellus hurried me through so fast that I had no time to read the names. What a place he lives in! I've never seen the like of it in all my life. Everything gold and marble and pictures and rugs and hundreds of slaves—the Emperor can't have any grander place, I'm sure. Tellus took me to a big room where his guests were, and they were a bit surprised when he brought me in. He introduced me as his young friend, and then all of them acted as though they were pleased to see me. They were wearing wreaths of flowers, which made them look awfully funny. Tellus invited me to dine with them, and said with a laugh: 'The dinner was planned for nine, but I guess we'll be ten for the while!' At once several slaves rushed up to me, took off my sandals, washed my feet, and stuck a wreath on my head. Tellus sat me on the middle couch as guest of honor; a slave tied a napkin around me and other slaves came with bowls and plates and gold spoons and knives, and still other slaves with the strangest foods you ever saw. People laughed because I didn't know how to eat the stuff, and they explained to me what the different things were and how I was supposed to eat them. There were flamingo tongues in wine sauce and wild-boar snout with truffles, and locusts in honey and frog's legs and mushrooms served in snow and awfully cold, and ostrich egg omelet and antelope roast, and on top of all that there were walnuts and apples and grapes and figs. After every bite I took, a slave wiped my mouth. One slave gave me a bowl of water; I thought I was supposed to drink it, but he whispered to me that I was to dip my fingers into it. I liked the way the different things tasted, especially the locusts; they were nice and crackly. Tellus told me he would have to discuss the letter with me later, but we never got around to that, because after the meal more wines were brought. They were all wines I've never heard of. White and yellow, heavy and light, and then some bitter stuff that was green. Tellus kept drinking to me and I drank to him, but

I could only sip the stuff, and then the men drank to me and I did some more sipping to them. The men started telling stories, and I had to tell a funny story, too, but I couldn't think of any, so I told how we found our teacher in the wardrobe, bound and gagged. They all roared with laughter about that, Tellus most of all. Suddenly there was music, a whole orchestra playing, but I couldn't see it because it was behind a curtain. Flutes trilling, harps and lyres twanging, trumpets singing out, and drums booming, and in between there would be a big crash as though somebody was smashing all the dishes, and they would all play at once. Then actors came in and recited something I didn't understand because it was in Greek. I can speak and read Greek in school, but I can't understand it. Dancers hopped around as though they all had stomachaches, but the clowns were awfully funny and I roared with laughter. But then laughing made me feel sick and everything started whirling in my head. And all of a sudden I remembered that maybe I wouldn't be able to read the names on the wall, and after that I didn't even dare sip any more wine."

"Why didn't you leave?" Flavius interrupted.

"I wanted to, but Tellus wouldn't let me go. Finally I pretended that I had to go out because I was going to be sick, and then they all laughed and

Tellus laughed, too, and told a slave to take me out. We went into the great hall and I stopped in front of the marble wall and tried to find the twentieth of March, but I couldn't find it. The slave started getting impatient, so I said I wanted to write my name down. I was trying to gain time. The slave gave a funny laugh and asked, 'Who do you think you are?' I said, 'Don't you know I am the guest of honor today?' And he said, 'But you're only a little boy.' So I shouted at him: 'What are you thinking of? I am not a little boy, I'm the Emperor's nephew.' That scared him and he ran off to get paint and a brush, and I felt good because I'd fooled him. I found the twentieth of March, but there were no names under it; the date was crossed out."

"Aha," Xantippus said. "The feast was canceled."

"And how did you get away?" Flavius and Caius could hardly wait to find out.

"I wanted to escape," Antonius continued, "but I was afraid the doorkeeper wouldn't let me out, so I ran down a corridor because I saw a garden at the end of it, but there were slaves in the garden so I ran back along the corridor, but there were more slaves coming from the other side, so I scooted into a room and closed the door. I wanted to climb out the window, but there were panes of glass in it. I heard voices on the other side of the door and thought of crawling under the bed—there was a big bed in the room, but it was too close to the floor and I couldn't squeeze under. So I hid behind a cloak hanging in a niche. I heard the slaves talking. One of them said, 'Maybe he is in there.' Another answered, 'You know the master has forbidden us on pain of death to enter his bedroom without permission.' 'But what shall we do if the boy is in there?' the first slave said. And the other said, 'Let us lock the door and go ask our master what to do.' They went away, and I thought: Now I'm going to be killed for entering here without permission. It was awfully exciting. I looked out from behind the cloak and bumped my nose against the chain. I recognized it at once and thought: Now I've got to get away, and I've got to take this cloak with me. So I wound it good and thick around my right arm, knocked out the window glass with it, and jumped. Luckily the window gave right on the street and I ran like mad." Antonius came to a breathless stop and stood looking at his friends like a victorious gladiator.

"You have done very well!" Xantippus praised him.

Antonius beamed.

Xantippus looked questioningly at his pupils. "Strange," he said. "How did the chain come to be fastened to Tellus' cloak? You boys had it last, didn't you?"

"We left it with Lukos when we ran away," Julius said.

"Then Tellus must have got it from Lukos," Xantippus said, shaking his head in puzzlement. "That means the two have dealings with each other. It also means that Lukos must have known who the owner of the chain was."

Xantippus looked the cloak over again. "It is a valuable camel-hair cloak," he said, unfolding it and weighing the fabric in his hand. "The kind ranking officers in the Orient usually wear. The chain also comes from the Orient, as you can tell by the hieroglyphs. Tellus spent many years in the Orient. There can be no doubt that the cloak belongs to him."

"Then it was Tellus who broke in here and attacked you!" Mucius said.

Xantippus raised his eyebrows. "As a rule, pensioned generals don't go in for burglary," he said. "But this is an exception, evidently."

"Perhaps someone borrowed the cloak from him," Julius suggested.

"People do not borrow cloaks from generals," Xantippus remarked. "The cloak belongs to Tellus. Incredible as it seems, he is our suspect. He also sent the courier to the newspaper. And why did he suddenly call off his banquet?"

"What can we do now?" Mucius asked.

Xantippus pondered and did not answer.

"We ought to accuse him publicly from the speaker's platform in the Forum," Julius said.

"We'll scream like the cranes of Ibycus," Antonius proposed.

"Or we'll write on all the walls: Ex-consul Tellus is the murderer of Rufus Praetonius," said Publius.

"But Rufus hasn't been murdered," Flavius objected.

"No matter," said Publius. "Anyone in prison is as good as dead."

"Give me my sandals, my cloak, and my stick," Xantippus said suddenly. "I know what I must do."

The boys brought him his things, and looked at him eagerly.

"I am going to see Tellus and tell him to his face that he is the evildoer," Xantippus declared resolutely.

"Aren't you afraid?" Flavius asked.

Xantippus' eyes flashed. "The man who desires the good must combat evil," he said grimly, and he began unwinding the bandage from his leg. Then he put on his sandals. "I shall ask him why he assaulted me, why he stole my writings on Pythagoras and my treatise on the acute angles of an obtuse triangle. I shall demand that he procure Rufus' release at once and threaten, if he refuses, to publish the whole story in the newspaper tomorrow morning. That will frighten him. Politicians fear public opinion beyond all else. Come on, help me into my cloak!"

Mucius and Julius draped the cloak around his shoulders. Xantippus took up his stick and straightened like a soldier coming to attention. "You wait here for me. If I am not back in two hours, inform the police." He started toward the door.

"Wait!" Mucius cried. "I have just thought of something."

Xantippus turned. "What is it?" he asked, frowning.

"Remember you told us that you struggled with the man who attacked you?" Mucius said, the words coming out in a rush.

Xantippus nodded impatiently. "Well?"

"Was the fellow tall or short?"

"Tall. Why? He was at least a head taller than I am."

"But Tellus is short," Mucius said. "Shorter than you."

"That's true," Antonius said. "He's small and fat and you are tall and thin."

Xantippus hesitated for a moment; then he came back into the room and sat down again. "Take off my cloak," he said. After a long pause he murmured: "Tellus is short—the burglar was tall—how is that possible?"

"A short man cannot be tall," Caius said.

Xantippus said nothing. The boys also were silent. Suddenly they heard footsteps in the classroom. Someone approached the curtain and remained standing behind it, breathing loudly.

"There's someone there," Flavius whispered.

"Someone where?" Xantippus asked, startled.

"Someone is at the door," Mucius said.

"Who's there?" Xantippus called sternly.

"Here I am," a gentle, deep voice replied, and an old man entered. He was dressed in rags, his bare feet covered by miserable shoes made of bark. Gravely he looked at Xantippus and the boys and said: "Greetings!"

"Greetings!" Xantippus replied. "Who are you?"

"Are you the pupils of the Xanthos School?" the old man asked.

"My name is Xanthos," Xantippus said.

"I come from prison and bring you a message from Rufus," the old man said in a slow, weary voice.

The boys instantly thronged around him, all saying at once, "From prison? How is Rufus?"

"Still living," the man replied. "I was fettered to him by the same chain." He raised his skinny arms and showed his wrists, bruised and swollen. "I was released today."

"Has Rufus been released also?" Mucius asked softly.

The old man shook his head sorrowfully. "No, he is waiting to be taken to trial, but nobody is paying the least attention to him. He lay beside me on the damp stone floor. We received almost nothing to eat or drink for days. But he has never cried—he's a brave boy. Only at night have I heard him sobbing."

The boys looked down at the floor.

"Were you able to talk to Rufus?" Xantippus asked, clearing his throat several times.

"Not often," the old man replied. "We were closely guarded, and no one is permitted to speak. You are beaten if you say so much as a word. When the guards came and removed my chains, Rufus sat up and looked pleadingly at me as though he wanted to say something but did not dare. Then, as I was being led out, he suddenly shouted after me: 'Go to the Xanthos School! Tell my friends they must tear the sheep's clothing off the red wolf.' That was all he could say, for a guard furiously lashed out at him with a stick. I came here at once to bring you his message. 'Tear the sheep's clothing off the red wolf!' What it means, you will know better than I. But make haste! It cannot be more frightful in Hades than it is in prison. Greetings!"

The old man bowed and left as suddenly as he had appeared. Xantippus and his pupils stared after him in perplexity. The meaning of Rufus' message was an utter mystery.

"We are to tear the sheep's clothing off the red wolf," Julius murmured. "What was he getting at?"

"That the red wolf is wearing sheep's clothing," Caius said.

"Idiot," Mucius rebuked him. "First we must know who he means by the red wolf."

All the boys looked hopefully at Xantippus. "Do you know who the wolf could be?" Mucius asked respectfully.

"I don't know anything about a wolf," their teacher replied.

"Why is the wolf red?" Flavius pondered.

"I don't know anything about a red wolf either," Xantippus said crossly.

"Maybe the sheep's clothing can help us somehow," Julius suggested cautiously.

"The wolf in sheep's clothing is an old fable," Xantippus replied. "We will be taking it up when school starts again."

The boys found little consolation in this reminder. They went on speculating.

"The red wolf is the culprit," Julius decided.

"But what has that to do with Tellus?" Mucius said. "Tellus isn't a red wolf."

"And Tellus is short, not tall," Caius reminded them.

"I can't understand why Rufus did not give us the right name," Publius said. "He must know it."

"Be quiet!" Xantippus interrupted them. "We must think this through step by step. Rufus did not say the real name because he did not want the guards to understand, for fear they would run and warn the criminal. That again proves that the culprit is an important personage. Rufus is still worried about his father. Not even the torments of prison would make him endanger his father's position. He must have spent a lot of time working out that message to us. The guards couldn't possibly know who was meant by the red wolf, but Rufus assumes we will see it immediately. Unfortunately we cannot, and therefore his message is of no help to us. We are in a blind alley. Let me think."

"It's maddening," Mucius said with a sigh, and

his words expressed the feelings of all the boys. It never occurred to him or to any of the others that the answer to the riddle lay right outside the window. The boys stared at Xantippus, waiting for some inspiration from him. But now even Xantippus was stumped.

It was growing darker outside, and violent gusts of wind rattled the shutters. Then it began to pour. Antonius went to the window and peered out unhappily. Suddenly he crouched down and called out in a low voice, "There's Tellus across the street!"

19

The Bakery

"Where?" the others cried, and were making a dash for the window when Antonius warned them back. "Keep down so that he won't see you."

They ducked down to the floor, crawled to the window and then peered cautiously over the sill. Xantippus, too, hugging the wall, had made his way to the window. "Where do you see him?" he asked.

"Over there!" Antonius whispered.

On the other side of the street a short fat man was walking rapidly in the direction of the Forum. He was wearing a cloak with a hood which he had drawn over his head.

"How do you know he is Tellus?" Mucius asked in a low voice.

"I recognized him right away," Antonius said. "His hood blew off for a moment and I saw his bald head and the scar. I'll swear it's him. He glanced over here, too, but he didn't see me."

"Probably he is going to visit Lukos," Xantippus murmured.

But Tellus walked past Lukos' house and stopped three houses further down the street, in front of a bakery. He turned around, took a long look at the Xanthos School and then vanished inside the baker's shop.

"He's gone to buy some rolls!" Flavius exclaimed in amazement.

Xantippus hobbled to his bed, sat down on it and began rubbing his leg. In straightening up from the floor he had moved too quickly and hurt himself again. The boys gathered around in concern, but the pain seemed to ease up. Then their teacher gave them his verdict. "A millionaire does not go out himself to buy rolls," he said. "In fact, he hardly goes anywhere without his slaves and hangers-on. All this is very suspicious. Perhaps Tellus has discovered the disappearance of the cloak and chain and is going to confer with somebody there."

"Meeting the red wolf!" Antonius exclaimed.

Xantippus shrugged. "Whoever it is, it would be interesting to find out what he is doing there."

"I'll run over and look," Mucius suggested.

"No," Xantippus said. "It would be dangerous for you to go alone. A cornered criminal will stop at nothing. It is better for you all to go together;

when there are six of you, you are much safer. But stick together all the time, and be careful. If you are threatened, get out. I don't want any foolish heroism!"

Mucius, Antonius, Caius, and Julius ran off, wild with enthusiasm. Publius followed them with a mocking expression; he thought nothing would come of this whole undertaking. As usual Flavius brought up the rear.

The cloudburst had turned the roadway into a rushing stream. The boys hopped across by way of the raised blocks of stone which were placed in the roadway at regular intervals, making a bridge from one sidewalk to the other for the use of pedestrians during just such storms as this. They raced down the sidewalk and charged into the bakery like the Persians into the pass at Thermopylae.

The baker, who was busy kneading some dough in a trough beside his oven, looked up in astonishment. "Hey, have you kids gone crazy?" he asked good-naturedly. "Are you planning to conquer Carthage for the second time? Or is school out?" He knew the boys well, for they were good customers of his. They always came around during the breakfast recess and bought piles of rolls and stacks of cookies.

Tellus was nowhere in sight. The boys went all

over the shop looking for him, while the baker watched them in wonder.

"Whatever became of that short fat man who was in here a while ago, the one in the hooded cloak?" Mucius asked.

The baker laughed. "Oh, him!" he replied, pointing to a door in the back of the shop. "He just went out through there."

"Why? What is he doing there?" Julius and Mucius burst out.

"He's a queer bird, he is," the baker said. He pulled the dough free from his arms and hands, tossed it back into the trough, and began kneading it again. "He comes through here three or four times a week. Comes in the front door and goes out the back."

"Why?" the boys chorused.

The baker shrugged. "Jupiter knows," he said indifferently.

"And that's all you know about him?" Mucius pressed.

"Absolutely," the baker assured him. "I don't ask him any questions. What do I care anyway. He pays me a hundred sesterces a month for the right to go through. I bet if he counted up his money he'd have more than all the rolls I ever baked in all my life. Once I made a mistake and asked him, 'Hey,

you in the hood, where in the world do you go to?'
And do you know what he did? He up and drew a
sword from under his cloak, glared at me like the
hellhound Cerberus and said, 'If you value your life,
don't think about it.' Since then I haven't thought
about it. I do value my life, even though I have to
wear myself out earning a living. I have a family to
support and a hundred sesterces a month isn't chick-
enfeed."

The boys stared at the back door.

"When does he come back?" Julius asked.

"Back?" the baker repeated. "By Pluto, he never
comes back! He comes in at the front, goes out at
the rear, but never returns."

Mucius went slowly toward the back door. "Where
does this lead to?" he asked.

"Nowhere," the baker replied. "That's the end
of the store."

"There must be something," Mucius said, pushing the door open slightly.

"You'd better not stick your head out," the baker
called to him. "First thing you know, he'll chop it
off with that sword of his."

But Mucius showed no sign of fear. He opened
the door further, leaned forward, and looked out to
both sides. The others came up behind him and
squeezed into the doorway, trying to see also. Before

them in the gray twilight lay a bare courtyard. About ten or twelve yards away rose a high wall. Beyond that must be the Field of Mars, for over the top of the wall they could see the crowns of cypress trees swaying in the wind. On their right the wall of the next building projected, so that they could not see where the yard ended.

"We ought to have a look around that corner at any rate," Mucius said.

"No harm in that," Julius murmured.

"Come on," Mucius said. They pulled their togas up to cover their heads and stepped out into the rain. Peering around the projecting wall, they saw that the yard extended as far as a high, massive building that stood at an angle to the other houses. There was no one in sight, and the boys boldly pressed forward. They stayed close to the walls of the buildings, paying no attention to the deep puddles. Where could Tellus have vanished to? The low houses adjoining the bakery had neither doors nor windows in the rear; Tellus could not have entered any of them. But then they came to a towerlike building made of heavy square stones, reaching high up above the one- and two-story shops. The boys realized at once that this was Lukos' house. To the left of it was the massive edifice of the Baths of Diana, the only other building around here of the same height. Between the two buildings yawned a narrow, dark gully. From Lukos' house a rectangular spot of light fell across this space and upon the wall of the Baths of Diana.

"There's a door open in Lukos' house," Julius said softly.

"Wait," Antonius whispered, and he crawled forward on hands and knees as far as the edge of the splash of light. Then he flattened out on his belly and squinted over the threshold. He withdrew his head hastily and crawled backwards to them.

"Tellus is in there," he reported.

"What is he doing?" Mucius asked.

"Nothing."

"Where is Lukos?" Flavius asked anxiously.

"I didn't see him," Antonius replied.

What was the next step? If the boys crossed in front of the door, Tellus would certainly see them. They stared indecisively into the dark gully, not daring to go forward and unwilling to go back. Then they noticed several thin rays of light in the wall about halfway between their observation post and the door. Mucius crept over to this light; then he beckoned the others to follow him. But he held a warning finger to his mouth.

The light came from a window over which heavy boards had been nailed. There were cracks between the boards, and the boys pressed their faces against the wet wood and peered through. The window was also protected with iron bars, but they could see directly into the big vaulted room in which they had been received by Lukos. It was darker than it had been when last they saw it, for there was no fire in the fireplace and the horrible masks on the pillars were not lit up either. A dim lantern was burning on the table at which Lukos had sat. The ceiling and the distant corners of the room were shrouded in dense shadows. On the table the boys spotted the basket of snakes, but it was covered over with a cloth. Next to it lay a short sword with a wide blade.

Tellus was sitting on a hassock and wiping the rain from his face. His cloak lay on the floor beside him. He seemed to be waiting for something, for now and then he tilted his head to one side and listened attentively.

"He's waiting for Lukos," Flavius breathed.

But suddenly Tellus jumped up, crossed the vaulted room rapidly and vanished behind a curtain which hung across a niche in one wall.

"There's another room," Caius said.

"Lukos is probably in there," Mucius declared.

"Or the red wolf," Antonius said.

"If only we could hear what they are saying," Mucius said impatiently.

But Tellus and Lukos remained behind the curtain. The boys could hear someone talking, but could not make out the words.

"I'll sneak over to the door and listen," Mucius said.

"I'm coming, too," Caius volunteered.

"So am I," Antonius said.

"Xantippus told us to keep together," Flavius complained.

"All right then," Mucius said. "We'll all go. Take off your sandals. If we make the slightest noise we're done for. Stick close behind me. If I call 'Watch out!', we all make a dash for it. Through the bakery, remember."

They slipped their sandals off, made a small heap of them next to the wall and stole up to the door. For a while they stared into the vaulted room. It remained empty, and Mucius led the way across the threshold. He walked on tiptoe, placing one foot ahead of the other very slowly, balancing himself with his arms. Every so often he paused and stood motionless, listening. The others followed his example. At last they reached the curtain and remained standing in front of it, holding their breath. From behind it they could hear a mysterious tinkling, metallic sound, and a hoarse voice murmuring, "One hundred, two hundred, three hundred . . ."

Mucius moved the curtain aside ever so slightly and found himself looking into a cellarlike chamber. The windowless stone walls glistened with dampness. On a small table stood a flickering candle that had almost burned down. Tellus was nowhere in sight, but Lukos sat with his back to the curtain. Mucius recognized him at once by his long, dirty-yellow hair and the black cloak with the silver stars sewn on it. The soothsayer was busy counting heaps of gold pieces which were stacked up on the table. As he finished with each stack he pushed it into a bag. He was completely absorbed in what he was doing, and went on murmuring, "Four hundred, five hundred, six hundred . . ." But suddenly he stopped and whirled around toward the curtain. His face was not painted black and white this time, instead he wore a clay mask tied over his face, the kind worn by actors on the stage. For a while he stared fixedly at the curtain, then he jumped to his feet. Frightened, Mucius let go of the curtain. "Watch out, let's run," he whispered sharply.

Flavius was the first to move; he shot toward the door as if he had been catapulted. But he tripped over a tight string stretched across the floor and fell forward on his face. Immediately the back door banged shut. The boys threw themselves against it in despair, tugging and pulling, but in vain.

"Don't bother," a hoarse voice said. "You won't get it open." Lukos had drawn the curtain aside and confronted the boys. They could see his eyes glittering evilly behind the clay mask. With clumsy footsteps he slowly approached them, and the boys instinctively moved closer together. Flavius was still stretched out on the floor, not moving. Either he was paralyzed by fright or playing dead.

Lukos went up to the fallen Flavius, stooped with a groan and pulled the boy by the hair.

"Help!" Flavius screamed piercingly; he sprang to his feet like a flash and fled toward his friends.

Lukos gave a short laugh. Then he sat down on the hassock, folded his arms and said menacingly, "I knew you were coming. You fell into the trap. This time you won't escape me."

"If you do anything to us, I'll tell my father," Caius said.

"You will never have the opportunity to tell your father anything again," Lukos replied.

A chilled silence followed. Finally Mucius cleared his throat and said somewhat hoarsely, "We don't want any trouble with you. We saw Tellus going in here."

"Tellus is not here," Lukos said sharply.

"Isn't he in there?" Mucius ventured, pointing to the curtain.

"Tellus has gone home," Lukos said. "A door in there leads to the side street."

"But his cloak is lying there," Julius said.

For a moment Lukos stared at the cloak lying beside the hassock. Then he croaked: "He was in a hurry to get home."

"Let us go home, too!" Flavius cried in a shaky voice.

"Oh no," Lukos said.

"You have no right to keep us here," Julius said defiantly.

"You have no right to come spying around here," Lukos replied mockingly. "People who pry into dangerous places must expect unpleasantness."

"We are not afraid. We are Romans," Mucius said heroically.

"Bravo, my son." Lukos chuckled. "You have no need to be afraid. I'm not going to hurt you."

That sounded a good deal pleasanter, and the boys breathed easier. Perhaps Lukos was not as bad as he pretended to be.

"You mustn't put a spell on us, either," Antonius said. "I know a lot better wizard than you. He'd take the spell off right away."

"I do not bother with enchantments," Lukos said tartly. "I can only see things that are hidden from other people. That is how I know why you are here.

2 1 0

You are looking for the desecrator of the temple.
You think he is Tellus."

The boys were taken aback. Lukos not only had
second sight; he could even read thoughts. Mucius
nodded assent. "We don't know for sure that it is
Tellus," he said. "But we suspect him. Perhaps it
was the red wolf. Do you happen to know who the
red wolf is?"

Lukos sat as though stunned for a moment; then
he suddenly jumped to his feet, waved his arms
wildly and screeched in a fury: "There is no red
wolf. Tellus is innocent. I am the desecrator of the
temple. I alone!"

20

Surprises

The boys stared incredulously at Lukos.

"So you don't believe me?" Lukos asked with a dangerous edge to his voice.

"But . . . the chain belongs to Tellus," Mucius managed to stammer.

"No!" Lukos screamed. "The chain and cloak belong to me. Tellus frequently visits me. I lent him the cloak."

"Tellus sent the courier to the newspaper," Julius murmured.

"He did it on my suggestion," Lukos said. "Tellus has nothing to do with the crime. You've been on the wrong track." He went to the table and hastily rummaged under the heap of papers. "Do you recognize that?" he asked, showing them a writing tablet. "This is Rufus' tablet. I'll tell you just how I copied his handwriting. I slit through the letters, pressed the tablet against the wall of the temple and painted over it with red paint. There, can you see it?" He held it in front of the lantern.

Showing up in thin illuminated letters on the writing tablet, were the words: *Caius is a Dumbbell.* The method by which the forging had been done was just what the boys had guessed.

"I also assaulted your teacher and stole the writing tablet from him," Lukos went on, shouting hoarsely. "Here are his books and pictures!" He tossed several rolls of parchment down at their feet. "Do you believe me now?"

The boys believed him. Lukos was also a head taller than Xantippus.

"Why have you done all this?" Mucius cried out. "Why were you so bent on hurting Rufus?"

"He discovered my greatest secret," Lukos said sternly. "He must die."

Filled with horror, the boys looked desperately around for a way to escape. But again Lukos seemed to guess their thoughts.

"Don't think you can run off to the prefect and repeat all this," he said mockingly. "Oh no, my dears. Tomorrow morning my ship leaves from Ostia. I shall sail back to my native land where I will be perfectly safe." He laughed scornfully. "And you will stay right here in this vault. You will never manage to open the doors; I alone know the secret mechanism." He took the sword from the table and with one powerful blow cut through the cords running across the floor. "There, now you can't get out at all. You can make all the racket you please—these walls are thick. No one lives back there and nobody ever passes. If you're lucky you'll be found; if not—well, that's your hard luck." Again he laughed maliciously.

Inwardly, Mucius was rejoicing. Lukos had not thought of the ladder leading to the roof. From there they could call for help. But he rejoiced too soon. Lukos considered for a moment. "No, you had better be locked up in the cellar," he said. He stopped and lifted a heavy wooden trapdoor in the floor. Beneath yawned a black opening, and the boys saw slippery stone steps leading down into the dark depths. "Come on, get down there!" Lukos howled. "Or I'll kill all of you."

Surprisingly, Mucius was the first to obey. He walked slowly toward the cellar steps. To reach them he had to pass close to Lukos. Suddenly he twisted around, gripped Lukos' arm with one hand and with the other tried to wrench the sword away from him. Lukos was taken by surprise for a moment. Then he defended himself wildly. But Mucius held on, knowing his life was now at stake. "Help!" he roared. The others awoke from their numbed daze and fell upon Lukos all at once. Like a pack of wild cats they gripped his arms and legs and tried to drag him to the ground. Lukos swayed back and forth. He succeeded in freeing one arm and struck Caius in the face with his clenched fist. Caius went down, but was instantly on his feet, and fighting mad. He seized the heavy stool in both hands, and brought it down with all his might on the back of Lukos' head. Lukos fell forward on his face and lay motionless with arms outstretched.

The boys were pale and breathing heavily.

"Bravo, Caius!" Mucius said, gasping for air.

Caius was still standing with the stool in his hands. His nose was bleeding and his eyes were ablaze with fury. "Shall I give him another?" he breathed.

"I think he's dead," Mucius said.

That was more than Caius had bargained for. "Dead?" he stammered.

"Dead?" Flavius repeated, shuddering.

"Come on, we've got to get out," Mucius urged them.

"Get out?" the others asked. "How can we?"

"The ladder," Mucius explained. "We'll climb up on the roof and call for help." He snatched up the lantern and ran into the long corridor which led to the front entrance. The others trotted after him.

The ladder stood in a niche beside the first door. By the dim glow of the lantern the boys could see ten or twelve rungs; the rest of the ladder was lost in the dim shadows above.

"That's pretty steep," Flavius murmured.

"Don't worry, I've been up on top already," Mucius encouraged him, and began climbing. The others followed close at his heels. But when they had reached about the middle, the foot of the ladder suddenly slipped backward, and the top slid down the wall at a rapidly increasing speed. Desperately, the boys clung to the rungs. Luckily the bottom struck the opposite wall of the corridor and the ladder came to a stop. The boys climbed back as far as they could and then jumped down to the floor.

"Boy, that might have turned out badly," Publius said with relief.

They tried to set the ladder up again, but it was jammed so tightly between the two walls that they could not budge it. After struggling desperately with it for a long time, they gave up.

They shook the door, drummed their fists against it, but here, too, their efforts were in vain.

"This is useless," Mucius decided. "Remember there's still another door beyond this one. No one can hear us."

They hurried back to the vaulted room and hammered against the rear door with every object they could pick up. They could not get at the shutters because of the iron bars over the window. Caius and Publius tugged wildly at the ends of the cords which Lukos had severed, but the door did not move.

"Wait!" Antonius said suddenly. "Remember Lukos spoke of another door in there, where Tellus went out." He pointed to the curtain in front of the niche.

They dashed into the chamber, and stopped in amazement. Four bare stone walls confronted them. There was neither door nor window. The candle on the table had burned down to almost nothing and was sputtering its last gasps.

"How could Tellus have gone out?" Mucius said slowly.

"Maybe there's a secret door," Julius said, and began tapping the walls. But as he approached a dark corner, he started back in fright. A fat toad was squatting on the floor, staring fixedly at him.

"That's Tellus," Antonius cried. "Lukos has changed him into a toad."

The others backed away slowly, throwing suspicious glances at the toad.

"Lukos said himself that he can't cast spells," Flavius whispered.

"He only said that so we wouldn't know Tellus

is the toad," Antonius said. "After all, it's a terrible crime to change anyone into a toad."

They returned to the vaulted room and slumped down discouraged on the floor, all in a row. They were tired and frightened, and their bare feet felt like lumps of ice. Lukos still lay motionless beside the cellar trapdoor, which had fallen shut during their scuffle. The mysterious disappearance of Tellus made their skin crawl. None of them quite believed Tellus had been changed into a toad, but still he seemed to have vanished into thin air. The lantern Mucius had placed on the table was growing steadily dimmer.

"Soon we'll be sitting in the dark," Mucius said, sighing. He drew up his knees and wrapped his cold feet in his toga.

Flavius, sitting at the end of their row, leaned forward and asked nervously, "How long will we have to wait until someone finds us?"

"Until we starve to death," Caius growled.

"It takes a while to starve," Julius said.

"So much the worse," said Publius with a short laugh.

"People can live for years on bread and water," Antonius said. "My father says that prisoners of war are given only bread and water, and they have to work besides."

"If only we had bread and water," Caius said. "I could eat ten loaves of bread right now."

"They say thirst is worse than hunger." Flavius whimpered.

"Stop that!" Mucius snapped at him. "Rufus has had nothing to eat or drink for three days and he is still alive."

"But he won't be for long," Publius said.

Julius regarded Lukos thoughtfully. "I should like to know what was that secret of his which Rufus discovered," he said. "Do you think it had something to do with the red wolf and the sheep's clothing?"

"Rufus must have been delirious when he said that," Publius suggested.

"That's right," Antonius agreed. "People say all kinds of things when they're starving to death. We once had a slave, an old man from Greece, who broke a bowl and was put in chains. He was given nothing to eat. I visited him and tried to cheer him up. He was so pleased he told me a funny story. The earth isn't flat, he said, but round as a ball. And it turns around the sun. I brought him food on the sly because I was sorry for him."

"He has a strange ring on his finger," said Julius, who was still staring at Lukos.

Antonius crawled closer to Lukos, and then cried

out in astonishment: "That's Tellus' seal ring. I saw the ring this afternoon on Tellus' finger."

"That's odd," Julius murmured.

"He must have stolen it from Tellus before he changed him into a toad," Antonius said. "What does a toad need a ring for, he must have thought. And look here!" Antonius exclaimed again. "See what Lukos has on his feet!"

The boys stooped forward curiously. The black cloak with the silver stars had slipped up and they could see that Lukos was wearing peculiar shoes with extremely high wooden soles.

"Those are cothurns," Julius said. "Actors wear them on the stage."

"So that's why he walked in that funny way," Mucius muttered to himself.

"But why is he wearing them?" Flavius asked.

"Aha!" Mucius exclaimed in sudden excitement, leaping to his feet.

Alarmed, the others jumped up also. "What is it?" they cried.

"What dumbbells we are," Mucius groaned. "What complete dumbbells! Now I know who the red wolf is!"

"Who?" the others demanded in feverish excitement.

"Lukos!" Mucius brought out the word like a

curse. "Lukos is the Greek word for wolf. Don't you remember the last list of Greek words we learned?"

"Of course!" Antonius seconded him.

"Ho lukos—the wolf!" the others repeated in chorus.

"But Lukos isn't red," Caius pondered.

"Not Lukos," Mucius said, "but remember the sign outside the door: the word LUKOS is painted in bright red letters. All we had to do was to look across the street and we would have realized at once what Rufus meant. Naturally he couldn't have known we would be so stupid. Even Xantippus was stupid."

"Ho lukos—the wolf," the others repeated, staring wide-eyed at the lifeless Lukos.

"But what about the sheep's clothing?" Publius asked.

"There!" Mucius said, pointing to Lukos' tangled, dirty-yellow hair. "That looks like sheep's wool." He stooped forward and gripped Lukos by the hair.

"What are you doing?" the others exclaimed.

"We are supposed to tear the sheep's clothing off him—you'll see in a minute," Mucius said with grim resolution.

"But you can't pull a dead man by the hair," Flavius protested in horror.

"I don't care," Mucius growled, and he pulled with all his strength. Suddenly something gave, and he was holding a wig in his hand. Underneath it appeared a bald pate with a large scar across it.

"Tellus!" the other boys shouted, incredulous.

"I suspected it," Mucius murmured. But he was really as surprised as the others.

21

Light

Tellus suddenly moved. The boys started back in fright.

"He's alive," Flavius whispered.

"The sword!" Julius cried.

Mucius stooped swiftly, picked up the sword that lay on the floor, and clasped it firmly in his right hand. With a groan Tellus sat up and gazed blearily at the boys. His fat face was smeared with blood. The clay mask had splintered as he hit the floor and the sharp pieces had cut him.

"Where am I?" he mumbled, and spat out a pebble he had been holding in his mouth. He had used the pebble, the boys realized, to disguise his way of speaking.

They stared fiercely at him. Tellus saw the sword in Mucius' hand and gave a weary gesture. "You don't have to be afraid, I won't touch you. I must have injured myself badly. Have mercy on me. Lean me against the wall!" His head drooped and he gasped for breath.

Caius and Antonius threw a questioning look at Mucius. Mucius nodded. "Go ahead, I'll keep an eye on him," he said, raising the sword.

Caius and Antonius lifted Tellus under the arms and dragged him back so that he had the wall for support. "Thank you," he murmured feebly. He gave them an imploring look. "Don't betray me. Have pity on me."

"You had no pity on Rufus," Julius said. "We must tell the police."

"You're good, sensible boys," Tellus pleaded. "I'll tell you everything—then you'll forgive me. Help me!"

"Help you!" Publius repeated sarcastically.

"Why did you pretend to be a soothsayer?" Antonius asked eagerly.

"Come closer!" Tellus whispered, rolling his eyes. "I can't speak any louder. I think I am dying."

The boys drew around him, but Mucius watched him closely. He felt uneasy about Tellus' mild tone.

"My spendthrift life has ruined me," Tellus began, speaking so softly that the boys had to lean forward in order to understand him. But as he continued his voice strengthened. "I had to borrow huge sums of money. My banker refused to lend me any more. My creditors threatened to sell me as a slave unless I paid them. That was two years ago. I could not flee, because they had me watched. I wanted to commit suicide, but suddenly I saw a way to obtain money again. Many years ago on one of my campaigns in the Far East I had taken prisoner a famous soothsayer named Lukos. He had made a fortune by his soothsaying, but he confessed to me that he was a swindler and could not really prophesy. He was an intimate of the King of Persia and acquainted with the king's secret plans. Consequently he knew in advance about important political events and skillfully used this knowledge. His prophecies almost always proved true, and the greatest men in Persia paid him enormous sums for telling them what the future held. So I decided to play the soothsayer also. I was an intimate of the Emperor, and what is the King of Persia compared to the Emperor of Rome! If Lukos could do it, I certainly could. So I established myself here as a soothsayer and was soon earning enough money to pay all my debts."

"When the Emperor finds that out, it won't be funny," Publius remarked.

Tellus nodded. "It was a dangerous business. For that reason I took all possible precautions to guard my secret. Everything was going well until Rufus caught me."

"Rufus?" the boys exclaimed.

"Rufus knew you were Lukos?" Julius asked.

"He discovered it by pure chance." Tellus sighed. "He came to see me night before last and told me about the writing tablet he had hung on the wall of the schoolroom, and about his fight with Caius."

"Why?" the boys asked.

"He wanted me to put a spell on his teacher," Tellus said.

The boys were still more surprised.

"What were you supposed to do?"

"I was to use magic to make his teacher forget to go to his mother next day."

"What a sly fox," Publius said.

"But how did Rufus know you were Tellus?" Mucius asked.

"It happened this way," Tellus continued. "I wasn't going to waste time on a boy, so I asked him for money. I took it for granted that he had none. That proved to be the case, and he went away very downcast. After he was gone, two other clients came to see me, but an hour later I started closing up, because I expected guests at my palace. I went into the next room, removed my wig and the makeup, but then returned to this room because I had forgotten my seal ring on the table. And suddenly there was Rufus standing in front of me. I had forgotten to use the secret mechanism to close the front door after the last visitor. Rufus had a purse of money in one hand and a lantern in the other . . ."

"That was my lantern," Mucius put in.

" 'Then you are Lukos!' Rufus exclaimed. He knew me because I often visited his father. I gripped his shoulder. 'If you betray me I will kill your father,' I threatened. I knew that the boy worships his father. 'You can't do that, my father is far away,' he said. 'Oh yes I can,' I said. 'Your father has just suffered a shameful defeat. If you don't swear to keep this to yourself, I'll see to it that the Senate recalls your father and has him executed. You know very well I have the power to do it. I only have to say a word to the Emperor.' I shook him roughly to intimidate him, and that must have frightened him too much, for he dropped the money, tore away from me, and ran out. As he ran his cloak slipped off. I wanted to follow him, but because of the cothurns on my feet I couldn't run fast."

"Why were you wearing the cothurns?" Flavius asked.

"As Lukos I wanted to seem very tall," Tellus said. "It also made me look thinner, so that it would never occur to anybody that I might be Tellus."

"And I suppose that's why you painted your face and wore the wig," Antonius said.

Tellus nodded. "I wore the clay mask only when I had no time to paint my face," he said.

"Did you find Rufus?" Mucius asked.

"No," Tellus said. "The door must have been open still and he escaped."

"The door couldn't have been open," Mucius said. "Otherwise he would not have escaped to the roof."

"To the roof?" Tellus asked in astonishment.

"I also fled to the roof because I couldn't get out," Mucius said.

"You?" Tellus asked. "But there's no way to get down from the roof."

"Yes there is," Mucius said. "We jumped across to the roof of the Baths of Diana and into the swimming pool."

Tellus stared at them. After a pause he asked cunningly, "But . . . but why didn't you escape to the roof just now?"

"We couldn't," Caius grumbled. "The ladder slid down and jammed."

The others were furious with him. Caius was so dumb. It would have been much better for Tellus to believe that they had a way to get out. Tellus, moreover, seemed to be relieved. He glanced toward the corridor, murmuring, "So you might have escaped that way."

"But why did you write 'Caius is a dumbbell' on the temple wall?" Julius asked.

Tellus wiped the blood from his face again. "I didn't think of anything of the sort at first," he said. "I felt fairly sure that Rufus would keep his mouth shut out of fear for his father. But almost as soon as he left another visitor came. I quickly put on my wig and the clay mask and let him in. It was a well-known senator, one who is feared for his sharp tongue. He had delivered a number of angry speeches against Praetonius in the Senate and had demanded his punishment on account of the defeat. He was highly excited. An hour before a friend who had just come from Gaul had visited him and told him that Praetonius had not been defeated, but had won a decisive victory. The official courier bearing the news of the victory had been held up en route, but would surely arrive at the Emperor's palace by the next day. The senator asked me to foretell whether he would fall into disgrace with the Emperor and whether he ought to take the precaution of going abroad. I told him it would be perfectly safe for him to stay. I knew the Emperor would not hold it amiss that the senator had desired the downfall of Praetonius because he is also jealous of Praetonius. The senator gave me a sack of gold pieces and went away jubilant. But I was in despair. Praetonius' victory was a disaster for me. The news of the victory would certainly be published next day, and then Rufus would no longer have any reason to fear my threat and would come out with his story. I had to silence him before he found out about his father's victory. But how? I racked my brains, and finally I thought of what Rufus had told me about the writing tablet and his quarrel with Caius. I saw that I would have to pin some crime on Rufus and get him arrested. Once the boy was in prison, he would no longer be able to talk. And I would arrange things so that he received no trial and was sent off promptly as a galley slave."

"Shame on you!" Flavius cried indignantly.

Tellus merely said, "If Rufus told my secret, I was done for. What would happen if the Emperor should learn that I had abused his trust in me?"

"He who does evil will reap evil," Julius said, remembering the maxims Xantippus had taught them.

"That is the truth," Tellus said. "But at the time I thought only of saving my own skin. I put on my old military cloak, which had been given to me as a present when I was serving in the Orient, and hurried over to the school. I knew the writing tablet must be hanging on one of the walls in the classroom. I felt along the walls, but in my excitement I had forgotten to take off the cothurns; they clattered when I walked and awakened your teacher, who came in. I struggled with him, threw him to the ground, picked up a stool and knocked him on the head. Then I tied and gagged him and locked him in the wardrobe."

"He would have suffocated if we had not found him," Mucius said reproachfully.

"I had to have him out of the way," Tellus said. "I wasn't able to find the writing tablet right off. Finally I found it in the chest."

"But why did you take the books and pictures?" Flavius inquired.

"That was to make it seem like an ordinary burglary," Tellus said.

"Oh, we noticed right off that something was fishy," Publius boasted.

"But why did you send the courier to the newspaper?" Julius wanted to know.

"Because I was afraid my plan might not work out," Tellus said. "The idea was to have Rufus arrested as soon as possible next morning. Perhaps the writing on the temple wall would not be discovered in time. Or else Vinicius might have tried to hush up the matter. A thousand things might interfere with a speedy arrest. So I thought of the newspaper story as a way of exerting pressure upon

Vinicius. I knew that Vinicius sends his copyist for the newspaper every morning. Therefore I pulled the hood low over my face, and before I went to the temple I delivered the story at the Censor's office. Had I waited until afterwards, the office would have been closed."

"That newspaper report was your big mistake," Mucius said.

"How so?"

"Because we figured out that it must have been written before the writing on the temple," Mucius explained. "That is how we first got on your trail. Otherwise we would never have suspected you."

Tellus looked crestfallen.

"Every criminal makes some mistake," Julius said. "You are no exception."

"But I had no choice," Tellus murmured. "As a matter of fact, even the newspaper notice would not have helped me if I hadn't denounced Rufus to the prefect myself."

"So that was your doing, too!" the boys cried, outraged.

"Yes," Tellus admitted. "Next morning I had myself taken to the Forum in a litter and waited near the prison to see for myself whether Rufus would be brought in. But as time passed and the sun rose higher and higher, I began to fear that something had interfered with the arrest."

"We did," Mucius said triumphantly.

"I grew more and more worried; before long, I knew, the news of the victory would be published. Finally I could stand it no longer; I ordered my bearers to take me to the prefect, and accused Rufus of the crime of blasphemy. I asked the prefect to keep my name secret out of consideration for the feelings of my friend Praetonius."

The boys were stunned by so much evil.

"You're a wicked man," Flavius said.

"What could I do?" Tellus said, and started groaning again as if he were suffering terrible pain. "Can't you understand what a frightful situation I was in?" He let his voice fade away to a whisper. But the boys were unmoved.

"Why didn't you run away?" Antonius asked.

"I didn't want to give up my comfortable life," Tellus said. "I would rather have killed myself."

"So you should have done," Mucius said contemptuously.

"That's easy to say," Tellus said. "Wait until you yourself are rich someday."

"When I am rich I will do only good," Mucius said with conviction.

"I suppose that after Rufus was in prison you

thought you were safe, didn't you?" Publius asked with a spiteful grin.

"Yes," Tellus said.

"You didn't reckon with us," Mucius said.

"No, not at first," Tellus admitted. "But after you came here with the chain, I began to be suspicious. I was taken by surprise, for I did not know I had dropped it. In my panic I lost my temper and threw you out."

"You also threw snakes at us!" Flavius reminded him.

"They aren't poisonous," Tellus said. "I only wanted to frighten you."

"Why do you keep the snakes?" Julius asked.

"I want the people who come to me to fear me."

"Humph, we weren't scared," Antonius boasted.

"Why didn't you throw the chain away?" Mucius asked.

"It's a good-luck token I was given in the East," Tellus replied.

"But it didn't bring you any luck," Publius pointed out.

"I fastened it to my cloak again and took it back to my palace. It seemed out of the question that anyone would ever find it there."

"But I found it," Antonius said. "What did you think when I came to see you?"

"I realized at once that the letter was only a pretext," Tellus said. "I wanted to get you drunk so that you would talk."

"I wasn't a bit drunk," Antonius said. "I didn't even really feel sick."

"When I discovered that my cloak was missing, I knew you were on my trail," Tellus said. "I counted on your observing me come in here, and laid my trap. I deliberately left the back door open to lure you in."

"You wanted to murder us," Antonius reproached him.

"No, not that," Tellus said. "I first wanted to find out whether you knew that I was Lukos. When I saw that you didn't know, I as Lukos took all the blame in order to clear Tellus. That is why I told you I was going back to my native land. I was going to lock you in here so that you would not be able to follow me and see where I was going. Lukos would have made his disappearance and Tellus would have been safe."

"Very cunning," Julius said. "But we would have gone to the prefect of the city and told him that Lukos is the criminal; we would have brought him here and shown him the writing tablet and Xantippus' books, and then Rufus would have been released and he would say you are Lukos."

"You would have been too late," Tellus said with a strange gleam in his eye. "Before coming here I went to the prison and bribed a guard to send Rufus to the galleys this very night. The ship is sailing early tomorrow morning and will be gone for at least a year. You will never see Rufus again."

The boys paled. Rufus would not long survive the grueling life of a galley slave.

"Murderer!" Mucius burst out.

Tellus gave a hypocritical sigh. "You should never have stuck your noses into my affairs," he said. "But you can still save Rufus," he added with a cunning look.

"How?" the boys cried.

"We'll make an agreement," Tellus said. "Let's leave it at that—that Lukos is the criminal and Tellus is innocent. If you swear you will not betray me, I will swear to send a messenger tonight to the captain of the galley with an order to release Rufus. The messenger can reach Ostia before the ship sails. But you must hurry. I know how to open the door. Let me out unharmed."

The boys hesitated. They did not trust Tellus.

"What do we do if you don't keep your word?" Julius asked.

"Then you can go to the police and inform on me," Tellus pointed out.

"But you're in no condition to walk," Flavius said. "How will you get home?"

Tellus considered for a moment. Then he said with a groan: "I'll let you out. Run to my palace and tell my slaves to come with a litter for me. Tell them Lukos tried to kill me and has fled."

The boys were in a quandary. If they went away, Tellus could destroy all the evidence of his double life as soothsayer, and could later deny everything. But there was little time to lose. If they were to save Rufus, they would have to decide on something.

"Give us a statement in writing that you acted the soothsayer Lukos and that you desecrated the temple," Julius said. "Then we'll let you go home."

"In writing? Why?" Tellus asked suspiciously. In spite of his bloodstained face they saw the veins in his forehead swelling.

"Because then if you don't keep your word, we'll take the statement to the Emperor," Julius said coolly.

Tellus considered. "What will you do when Rufus is free?" he asked.

"We'll give the statement back to you. We swear that we will not betray you."

The others were proud of Julius. This was brilliant thinking on his part. Once they had the statement, Tellus could not cheat them. But he would have to hurry, for the light of the lantern was growing steadily dimmer and they were very much afraid it would be dark before they could leave. Fortunately, Tellus seemed unaware of the failing lantern. "Give me pen, ink, and paper from my desk over there," he said. "I'll write whatever you say." He leaned back against the wall, eyes half closed, as though he were totally done in and no longer had the strength to object.

Publius and Antonius brought Tellus paper, a reed pen, and ink. They knelt down at his side; Antonius handed him the paper and pen, and Publius held the ink. Tellus wrote swiftly; then he started to hand the statement to Antonius, but Julius called out: "Press your seal underneath for signature. Otherwise people might think it wasn't genuine."

Obediently Tellus pressed his seal ring into the papyrus.

Satisfied, Julius took the statement and read it aloud to the others: "I, Marius Clodius Tellus, Ex-consul and victorious general, hereby confess that I pretended to be the soothsayer Lukos and wrote 'Caius is a dumbbell' on the wall of the temple of Minerva. Rufus Praetonius is innocent."

"Fine," Julius said. "And now tell us quickly how to open the door. We'll run over to your palace and send your slaves here."

Tellus eyed Mucius and said, "First you must swear."

"We swear . . ." Julius started to say.

"No, you must all lift your right hands," Tellus murmured feebly. His eyes were almost shut now.

The boys raised their right hands. Mucius hesitated, watching Tellus narrowly. But the man was drooping against the wall as if he were at the end of his strength. There was nothing to fear from Tellus. Mucius shifted the sword to his left hand in order to raise his right hand, but at that moment Tellus sprang forward, snatching at the sword. Mucius leaped back in a flash and pressed the tip of the sword against Tellus' chest, shouting: "One move and I'll run you through!"

Tellus froze where he was, on his knees, staring with hate-filled eyes at Mucius. Suddenly the light went out. In the darkness the boys stood numbed with fright. They heard Tellus jump up and make off, his high wooden shoes clattering against the floor. Then there was a brief silence. It was broken by several thunderous blows against the rear door and a confusion of excited voices in the yard.

"Help!" the boys shrieked.

"Open the door!" someone outside commanded.

"We can't!" the boys shouted. "We're locked in."

Three more powerful blows followed. The door

splintered and cracked at the joints. In the opening appeared several Praetorians holding a battering ram. Back of them stood others with torches and drawn swords, their chest armor glittering in the glow of the torches. The Praetorians finished smashing the door and the soldiers stormed into the vaulted room.

Close behind the soldiers appeared two officers with high plumed helmets, and then Vinicius in flowing senatorial toga, a long sword in his hand. Finally Xantippus squeezed through the ruins of the door. He was dripping wet. Waving his stick wildly, he shouted, "Where are they?"

"Here!" the boys roared enthusiastically. "Hurrah for Xantippus!"

"The gods be praised, you're alive!" Xantippus said, overjoyed.

"Of course we're alive," Antonius said.

"What is going on here?" Vinicius asked, looking inquiringly at his son.

"Nothing in particular," said Caius with great calm.

"Tellus is Lukos," the others shouted. Julius handed the statement to Vinicius, who read it in amazement. "By Jupiter, that is almost unbelievable. Tellus is Lukos!" Suddenly he seemed to realize the meaning of the words, and his eyes flashed fire. "Where is he, the criminal!" he cried.

"He's hiding somewhere," the boys said.

"Find him!" Vinicius ordered the soldiers. The Praetorians separated. Some ran into the adjoining chamber, two descended into the cellar, and others disappeared down the long corridor. From there one called, "He's escaped to the roof."

"Follow him!" Vinicius shouted, and they all ran into the corridor. The ladder was standing upright again. In his desperation Tellus had summoned up strength to free it. Some of the soldiers had already climbed to the roof and called down, "He has disappeared."

"Then he's jumped into the Baths of Diana!" Mucius shouted. "Follow me." He raced back down the corridor.

"Take the battering ram with you!" Vinicius called to the soldiers.

They ran across the yard, through the bakery, down Broad Street, and into the side street to the front entrance of the Baths of Diana. The soldiers broke in the door and they all rushed inside.

Tellus lay on the floor of the swimming pool. There was no longer any water in it.

Vinicius descended the steps to where he lay and bent over him. Then he straightened up. "He is dead."

There was a moment's silence. Only the beat of the rain on the roof and the low crackling of the burning torches could be heard. The boys stared wide-eyed at Tellus in the empty pool.

"He jumped too late," Mucius murmured.

22

The Banks of the Rhine

Xantippus stood up and tapped the knuckle of his middle finger on his desk. "Attention!" he ordered.

The boys fell silent, straightened up, and looked at him attentively. But inwardly they were sighing. Their vacation was over, and with it their adventure. Life was dull again. Outside the sun was shining, and people were hurrying by with happy faces; spring had come with full force. But what good was it? School came first; spring had to wait.

They sneaked glances outside. Across the street on Lukos' house there still hung the sign: LUKOS, WORLD-FAMOUS ASTROLOGIST . . . But one of the Xanthos pupils had drawn two heavy charcoal lines across the bright-red letters and had written below: *Moved to Hades.*

Three days had passed since Tellus moved to Hades, and school was starting again. The boys were all present. Rufus sat on his usual bench. He still looked rather pale and worn, but he had recovered from the horrors of prison with amazing speed. The only marks he bore of his experience were the swellings on his wrists and ankles, where the chains had been fastened. Immediately after Tellus' death Vinicius, Xantippus, and the boys had gone to prison and released him—in the nick of time, moreover, for he was just about to be taken away secretly. The guard Tellus had bribed was himself put in chains for breaking the law. For according to law no Roman citizen could be punished unless a formal sentence had been passed in court. Then Rufus had been taken home in triumph by his friends, and his mother Livia had wept for joy.

Once again Xantippus tapped on the top of his desk. "My dear pupils," he began solemnly, "you have done your work well. As I have told you time and again, persistence will lead you to your goal. But now I must ask you to apply yourselves to your studies with the same determination you so successfully used to rescue your friend Rufus. The task of the hour is: work and learn! Tellus' frightful fate should serve as a lesson. The path of vice leads inevitably to ruin."

Caius yawned aloud. Xantippus' speeches always made him sleepy.

"I must ask you to suppress all unnecessary

noises," Xantippus said, pausing until there was complete silence again. Then he continued: "We are all very glad that Rufus is back with us."

Rufus bowed, and his friends could not help laughing. Xantippus went on in a louder voice. "For a time it seemed that we might never see him again. But the gods were gracious to us. We all enjoyed the wonderful party at Livia's. We have brought offerings of gratitude to the household gods; we have made speeches, sung songs, and played games; and we have all eaten very well indeed. All your parents were present and I had the honor to be your guest."

"Claudia was there, too," Rufus added.

"I know," Xantippus said, and he narrowed his eyes with just the faintest suggestion of a smile. "Claudia is a well-bred little girl. She is not the type of child, I think, who tries to have a spell put on her teacher."

Rufus flushed. The others grinned.

"But I, too, have made mistakes," Xantippus said. "I allowed myself to be carried away by anger. That was unbecoming a teacher, and I regret it. I hope that from now on we will understand one another better. But do not imagine you can get away with laziness on that account. Now more than ever I must ask of you hard work and perfect conduct.

In mathematics we shall finish up with Pythagoras, and then turn to the study of Archimedes, Euclid, and others. In Greek I am thinking of getting to Homer, Aeschylos, Sophocles, and Euripides. For history I have in mind at the moment Pliny and Livy."

Hearing this, the boys found it rather hard to look forward hopefully to the future. They pulled long faces, but Xantippus went on serenely: "In order to round out our program, we shall not neglect the study of the earth and its peoples. And today, my young friends, we might well begin with geography. Praetonius' great victory over the rebellious Gauls provides us with a golden opportunity to take a closer look at the country where the battle took place, and at the peoples that inhabit it. Who remembers what I taught you about the Gauls last time? Antonius!"

"Present!" Antonius blurted out, jumping up nervously. He had just slipped Publius a writing tablet on which he had scribbled: "We should have left Xantippus locked in the wardrobe."

"Well, my son," Xantippus said, "what do you know about the Gauls?"

"Lots," Antonius answered with gusto. "We once had a slave who was a Gaul. He was supposed to wash the windows, but he had never seen glass and spent the whole day staring through the glass instead of washing it. My father sold him cheap."

"That is not to the point," Xantippus said reprovingly. He took his stick from the desk and went over to the map which hung on the wall. He was no longer limping. "Look here," he said, pointing to a spot on the map. "This is Gaul. The Gauls had assembled in vastly superior numbers on the left bank of the Rhine in order to fall upon Praetonius and his legions. Praetonius withdrew to the right bank, and the Gauls celebrated, thinking they had forced him to retreat. But during the night Praetonius returned undetected and almost annihilated the army of the Gauls. Here, where my stick is pointing, is the Rhine. The Rhine is a mighty river. On both sides of it live hostile peoples. On the left bank the Gauls live, and on the right the Germans." He paused and called out angrily, "Caius!"

Caius started, for he had been dozing.

"Repeat what I have just said," Xantippus ordered.

"The Rhine . . . the Rhine . . ." Caius stammered helplessly. "The Rhine is a river that has banks on both sides."

The others roared with laughter.

"Quiet!" Xantippus thundered. The boys fell silent and waited resignedly for the long lecture that was as sure to follow as day follows night.

But suddenly a miracle happened. Xantippus began to laugh.

The boys were thunderstruck; they had never seen their teacher laugh before. Xantippus laughed until the tears ran down his cheeks. When his laughter began to subside, he wiped his eyes and said, still chuckling: "Caius, you really are a dumbbell!"